QUEEN OF HEARTS

FAMILY STONE #6 SHELLEY

LISA HUGHEY

LISA HUGHEY

QUEEN OF HEARTS

by

Lisa Hughey

December 2014

Lisa Hughey

ISBN: 978-0-9903793-5-5

Print ISBN: 978-1-950359-00-4

ALL RIGHTS RESERVED. This book contains material protected under International and Federal Copyright Laws and Treaties. Any unauthorized reprint or use of this material is prohibited. No part of this book may be reproduced or transmitted in any form or by any means, electronic or mechanical, including photocopying, recording or by any information storage and retrieval system without express written consent from the author/publisher.

This book is a work of fiction and any resemblance to persons living or dead, or places, events or locales is purely coincidental. The characters are products of the author's imagination and used fictitiously.

ISBN: 978-0-9903793-5-5

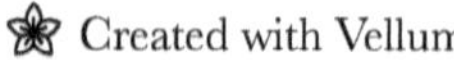 Created with Vellum

CHAPTER 1

*C*ould she be more out of place?

Shelley Stone sat at the end of the ultra-trendy bar. Blue neon and soft white uplights glowed, spreading over the wall behind the display of upscale liquor bottles, and giving the AquaKnox bar a fuzzy, almost surreal ambiance with a dash of sophistication. Shelley scanned the drink menu and people-watched as she waited for the rest of her party to arrive.

Despite the fact that she lived in a mansion in Monterey, and had a portfolio that rivaled Warren Buffet's, she had never embraced a hedonistic or sophisticated lifestyle.

She was more at home in a pair of Capri jeans and cotton halter top than the dressy, formal attire she wore now. Her LBD was subtly sexy, with matching V's in both front and back, revealing a discreet amount of cleavage. The skirt hit above her knees. Not so far above as to be indecent but short enough that she bared a sleek amount of toned, tanned leg.

She wasn't quite sure how she let Bliss talk her into this dress.

Her soon-to-be daughter-in-law could be quite persuasive.

On the outside, Shelley looked like she belonged. But on the inside, she was still that naïve kid from Wisconsin, who with starry-eyed innocence searched for a man to make all her problems disappear.

Instead, the man had given her more problems, then disappeared himself.

Shelley sighed.

She ordered a Lemon Drop martini from the handsome, younger bartender. He gave her an assessing once over before granting her an intimate smile. "How's your evening so far?"

She let a jaded cynicism shadow her eyes. "Just fine."

In truth, her evening was weird. Her son was getting married. Jack wasn't really her son, but her stepson, who was only ten years younger than Shelley. God, how was it possible that at the end of the week she was going to be the mother of the groom?

Shelley looked more like Jack's older sister. But in every way that mattered, Jack was her son.

She was damn proud of the man he'd become.

The bartender took the brush off philosophically. "If you change your mind, I'm off at eleven." His smile promised decadent things. Hot, sexy, naughty things that she hadn't experienced in a good long while.

"Thanks, but I'm good."

"I bet you could be a lot better." He lightly flirted. Not enough to be offensive, but clear enough that if she wanted to she could probably hook up with him when he got off work. Except he left her cold.

Besides the fact that he was younger than her adopted

sons, she wasn't attracted to the muscle-bound bartender. At all.

Someone brushed by her seat, so close, the hint of clean soap and bracing aftershave tantalized her senses. Heat skittered along the bare skin of her back. And she couldn't help but turn to see who initiated that reaction. He had a broad chest laden with muscles, wide shoulders, a flat stomach, thick shiny black hair with a few threads of silver, and the healthy glow of the physically fit on his dark-skinned, likely Hispanic, face. He languidly sat on one of the barstools three down from her. His magnetism was like a force field, and Shelley had to consciously avert her gaze.

The heat the bartender had been trying to generate was a flicker compared to the surge of attraction this guy caused. Her response was so intense, Shelley flushed.

Shelley purposely kept her attention on the tart drink in front of her.

Within a minute, two overly made up and overly bare twenty-somethings started chatting up the hot, older guy. She was too old compared to the sexy, young girls who were trying to pick up the man. They were clearly looking for a sugar daddy. She wanted to offer them some hard-fought, well-intentioned advice…*Don't do it.*

But she knew they wouldn't heed her warning.

She sure hadn't listened to her mother. Which was how she ended up pregnant and alone at eighteen.

The older sophisticated man who'd swept her off her feet, at least it felt like it at the time, had dropped her ass the second he'd found out she was knocked up. While she'd been devastated at the time, looking back on it now, she was grateful that Jack Stone Sr. had dumped her.

She had been forced to become strong and learn to take care of herself.

Jackson Stone Sr. was a class A bastard who left a trail of women behind him.

The best day of Shelley's life had been going to the Stone mansion and becoming mother to Jack's boys as well as her own daughter, Jess.

Now her babies were all grown up. In the past few months, all four of her kids had found partners. She approved of her kids' choices, and believed they had chosen well. She was so thrilled for them. Happy they'd found companions to share the ups and downs of life.

But since they'd all become couples, *her life* felt more empty than before.

They were all in Las Vegas for a weeklong family vacation and celebration before Jack and Bliss got married.

Connor and Ava, Jess and Colin were already here. Riley and Di would be here in the next few days. Couples everywhere she looked.

Except for her.

She'd come down to the restaurant a little before their family dinner was supposed to begin, to give herself time to gather her thoughts. She didn't want the sadness that had plagued her lately to overshadow Jack and Bliss's wedding trip.

Shelley picked up her martini, gave herself a slight tip of the glass to toast successfully raising four kids and then took a sip of the sweet-tart, strong drink. A small, bittersweet smile curved her lips. Four kids.

Damn. She had moments where she felt about a hundred years old. While she wouldn't trade one moment of the last twenty years for a footloose and fancy free life, melancholy for the loss of her youth hit hard. She'd gladly forsaken her immediate future to raise four kids. But now what did she do?

Her glance shot to the too young women again and she rolled her eyes. Good luck, girls. She'd been cured of that starry eyed innocence in about fifteen seconds when Jackson Stone Senior had told her to get rid of her baby.

She could still remember that visceral shock to her heart when he'd calmly handed her money and said he never wanted to see her again. She'd numbly taken the handout, even though she had no intention of aborting her baby. She'd not been aggressive, she'd just gone away.

Jess had been the first of many blessings in her life. The best decision she'd ever made had been walking away from Jack Sr. The second had been coming back.

Now all her 'kids' had found their soulmates.

Most days, Shelley had no belief in love and forever. But she'd never shared her feelings on the subject with her kids. They had to make their own mistakes, their own decisions. She couldn't fault that all four had found extraordinary people to share their lives with and she hoped with all her heart that they found nothing but joy together. They deserved every drop of happiness they could eke out of life.

However their love had unleashed a long buried wish for that same kind of closeness with a man. Her young romantic soul had been crushed by years of struggle. Sex had been number one hundred and one on her priority list. She might not believe in forever love, but she'd sure like to experience some physical, temporary sex.

She'd watched the father of her child run through women like a bowling ball through pins. He'd also managed to alienate his entire family along the way. Thankfully, nowadays Jackson left them alone.

He had certainly managed to get more than his fair share of sex while Shelley had been basically celibate at home. She'd dated several men in the last few years. Nice, debonair older men. The kind who hadn't helped raise their own kids and were searching for wife number three. What was wrong with her that men her own age wanted nothing to do with her?

She was thrilled that her children had found happiness and love. But she knew she was destined to be alone.

ENRIQUE "BULLETPROOF" Santana, Ric to his friends, BP to his men, raised a surprised brow at the blatant come on from the hot, young, make that barely legal woman, who'd approached him as soon as he sat down to wait for his friend on the bar stool at AquaKnox.

"You in the mood to party?" The brunette ran one neon pink, polished nail down the placket of his white Polo shirt.

"We're available." Her friend who was almost identical except her hair color was blonde, crowded close to his other side and let her surgically enhanced breasts rub against his bicep.

They were gorgeous, no question, all tanned long legs, large fake breasts, and puffy lips slicked with bright gloss that matched their nails. Their dresses revealed as much as they concealed, in bright geometric patterns with strategic cutouts, and spike heels that could double as lethal weapons.

But he wasn't interested in the sure things.

He was likely crazy, because his attention kept returning to the sleek woman at the end of the bar like a heat seeking missile targeting infrared radiation. She exuded a subtle sexuality that was far more appealing than the obvious charms of the two girls next to him. The woman at the end of the bar had some mileage, she was probably close to his age, but she wore it well. More than well. Fantastically.

He'd been feeling less than content lately. As if something were missing in his life. He'd accomplished his career goals, achieved the rank of Commander in the Navy before he retired to form his own company.

His choice of companion had definitely gotten younger as he'd gotten older, mostly because women his age tended to be married with kids, or divorced and bitter. However, he found himself ignoring the unsubtle chicks in favor of the older, more seasoned woman, and that surprised him.

When the woman at the end of the bar pursed her red slicked lips over the edge of the martini glass, his cock stiffened at the lush promise of her mouth. She exuded an understated sex appeal that was all the more attractive because she wasn't trying at all.

The sugar from the rim coated her lips and all he could think about was licking those crystals from her mouth, then having her mouth pucker over something more personal.

She didn't have that frantic air of desperation that hovered most of the women he met these days. Or the calculated eagerness that he detected in the wide-eyed gazes of the young women who continued to run their soft, pampered hands with their sharp colorful nails along his chest.

These girls were searching for the bonus, figuring out how they could get ahead from the encounter. Versus the woman at the end of the bar who wasn't even in the game.

Ric carefully grasped the brunette's hand and lifted it away from his body. "Excuse me, ladies." He walked between the nubile babe sandwich without a backward glance.

Life was too short to waste time. When he knew what he wanted, he went after it. His problem lately was he had no freaking idea what he wanted.

Until *she* sat down at this bar.

Suddenly all he wanted was her.

He had a commitment tonight. He could bail. As long as he was at the ceremony in a few days, his buddy would understand his compulsion to snatch this woman up and take her for a ride. Before he'd abruptly turned into a taken man, his former SEAL teammate had been just as willing to avail himself of a hot woman as Ric.

He prowled toward the woman tucked away at the end of the bar. She glanced over just as her pink tongue swiped at the sugar-frosted rim of her martini glass. An unexpected flush rose from the deep V of her neckline, her breasts demurely showcased by the black little black dress. The blush spread over her face as she intuited his predatory intent.

She started to hunch, then determinedly squared her shoulders and deliberately shifted her attention to the glowing blue wall behind the bar. Water cascaded down the glass wall and shimmered in the subtle lighting.

"Is this seat taken?" He spoke directly to her, forcing her to acknowledge him. His voice deepened as he leaned closer and inhaled her sexy, earthy scent. Up close, her skin glowed with a healthy tan. Her inner exuberance for life completely overshadowed that subdued, demure façade.

She lifted her vibrant green gaze and held his for one long moment. The she dropped the thick fringe of her dark lashes and shrugged. "Knock yourself out."

"Ric." He held out his hand, knowing she'd take it. Her good manners would force her to shake even if she wanted to avoid him.

"Shelley." Her voice was husky as he slid his palm against hers. The shock of electricity was instantaneous and physically visceral. A bolt of attraction zinged straight to his cock. He couldn't remember the last time he'd had such an incendiary reaction to a mere brush of hands.

Instant lust. Damn. He wanted her.

Now. For hours. If just the touch of her hand evoked this kind of physical reaction, he couldn't begin to imagine what would happen when he covered her body with his and drove home. Just thinking about it hardened his cock into a club.

Her hand was small and delicate in his, but not soft. She had some calluses as if she were unafraid of hard work. The contrast was highly intriguing.

Which enthralled him even more.

She snatched her fingers away. Goose bumps peppered her arms and her nipples poked the black silky fabric. Ric suppressed a wickedly satisfied grin. Oh yeah. She was as affected as he was.

He knew had to proceed carefully or she would bolt.

"Can I buy you a drink?"

"No, thanks."

Ric raised his index finger to signal the bartender. When he sauntered over his face was set in an annoyed frown. "I'll have another Sam Adams. And can you please put the lady's drink on my tab?"

"It's already taken care of," the bartender responded shortly. Ric had seen him hit on the woman earlier, clearly her sex appeal wasn't limited to forty-year-old guys. Because the bartender was easily ten years younger than her. Possibly more.

Ric understood the bartender's animosity but no way was he going to let this kid win. His life's strategy had served him well. She was his. Win at all costs.

She jerked. "But—"

"It's already taken care of," the bartender said again firmly.

Her smile lightened her face and brightened her moss green eyes. "Thank you."

The bartender glared at Ric before speaking to Shelley. "My pleasure."

"What brings you to Las Vegas?" Ric propped his elbow on the clear bar with lights embedded in the Lucite, and turned his back to the bartender effectively cutting him off and enclosing them in a private circle of two.

"Look. I'm sure you're a perfectly nice man."

Nice. The kiss of death. Ric suppressed the urge to snort. He wasn't nice. But he also didn't want to scare her.

"I can be not so nice," he said silkily. The insinuation registered in her small inhalation of breath. Not giving her time to complete the brush off, he leaned so close he could see the dilation of her pupil as her body reacted to his words. Clearly he'd sparked a chemical reaction and she was thinking of something not so nice too.

Hoo-yah, she was as affected as he was.

Her skin warmed and her scent, something floral with a hint of earthy musk, heated and surrounded him. God damn, he could just eat her up. Her breath caught at their combined heat and the promise in his eyes. He wanted her. Wanted to spend the night with her, exploring all her sweet feminine places. Her hand fluttered at the base of her neck where her pulse beat rapidly in her throat. Her tongue came out again, this time to lick at her lips. Ric nearly groaned. He'd never had this kind of primitive reaction to a woman in his life.

She might be saying not interested, no thank you, but her body was giving him a completely different message. *Come and get me.*

He wanted to fist pump in triumph, but he kept his reaction under wraps.

"I—"

"No games." He didn't want to waste time on some sexual dance that was half seduction, half innuendo, but all fake. He wanted to press up against her. Wanted to show her without words how much he wanted her. "I am insanely attracted to you."

She rolled her eyes. He could tell she was getting ready to blow him off. And God, for the first time in his life, the thought of begging didn't fill him with disgust. He was ready to get down on his knees and plead with her to spend time with him.

"I think you'd have better luck with your previous companions. I'm sure you can catch them if you run." She dismissed him with a cool smile and feigned disinterest. Except the flush across her chest and face had deepened and her pupils had dilated nearly encompassing the bright green of her iris.

His body seized with almost frantic desperation. She was trying to shut him down. His entire endorphin system was going haywire, as if an EMP had wiped out every cogent thought except one. Get closer to her.

"I don't want them." If he didn't get to touch her, he would expire on the spot. "I want you."

"Eeep." She gulped down the martini, her lips pursed against the glass rim, and Ric's entire body froze, paralyzed with lust.

"I'm not bluffing." The rough edge to his voice had her leaning back.

"Um." Her painted fingernails pushed the almost empty martini glass between them as if she could create a barrier to protect herself. But she couldn't protect herself from her own body's reaction to the pheromone cocktail that was making him dizzy and drunk on her.

Ric's heart thudded with an unrelenting sense of panic. He couldn't stand it if she shut him out.

"Problem here?" The bartender interrupted.

Ric responded quickly, "No."

"Not at all," she replied politely and shot the bartender a bland, half smile before turning to address Ric. "You certainly are direct."

"I'm old enough to know what I want and go after it." Ric slid closer to her and yes! she didn't back away. Her tongue came out and licked the sugar that dusted her mouth.

"My," she said faintly.

She clearly wasn't used to the honest approach or the fact that he considered her sexy. But damn, his body was on fire.

"Have dinner with me." He curled his fingers over her free hand, the one resting on her bare knee. "Let's get to know each other better."

What he wanted to say was, *Come back to my room with me. Let me feast on your curves and learn every erogenous zone on your delicious form. Let me worship your body and discover your secret places and subtle turn ons.*

But as skittish as she was, if he confessed what he wanted to do to her, she'd rabbit. And in this monstrosity of a hotel, he'd never see her again.

"I have plans," she said huskily.

"So do I." He threaded his fingers through hers. Her hand was cool to the touch but a fire burned beneath her prim dress and her lowered lashes. She was thinking about it. "But I'd rather make new plans."

He wanted to push harder. Being passive wasn't in his

nature. But instinctively Ric knew if he didn't back off some he'd lose the opportunity. He hadn't made O-6 pay grade because he'd been tentative or indecisive. He'd risen through the ranks of the Navy because he'd been a creative problem solver.

"I'm sure you could find an easier…dinner companion," she demurred. Still trying to deny their attraction.

"I look at obstacles as opportunities."

She laughed breathlessly. Her fingers tensed under his, as he carefully stroked his index finger over the back of her hand. And he prayed that she'd throw caution to the wind and agree to have dinner with him.

He was so close he could see the striations of green in her eyes along with her clear longing to leap. "No strings."

She raised one perfectly groomed auburn eyebrow as if to say, really?

He kept up the honesty. "Didn't say I don't want there to be strings. Just that I won't attach any to dinner."

She traced the rim of her almost empty martini glass with one French-manicured nail. Her shoulders had hunched slightly and he knew she was getting ready to say no.

"Take a chance." Ric urged. "Throw the dice. It's Vegas."

Acquiescence flowed over her body like a wave crashing on the shore of Coronado. "Where are we going to dinner?"

For some reason, Ric felt as if he'd already won the war. "Follow me."

CHAPTER 2

*R*ic. The insanely hot man who'd just asked her to so much more than dinner lead her away from the bar, his fingers curled around hers loosely. She might be inexperienced but she wasn't stupid.

Shelley tried not to shiver but her body was lit up like the neon flashing, frenetic lights of the Strip and she buzzed with adrenaline and the anticipation of doing something wicked. She was so far outside her comfort zone right now she might never find her way back to the settled land of easy and comfortable.

As he rubbed his thumb over the sensitive valley in her palm, Shelley wasn't sure she cared.

Her heart beat in her chest, pounding out an uneven rhythm as she realized that for the first time in years she was doing something strictly for herself. His forearm, muscled and thick and dusted with dark hair, brushed against hers, causing a cascade of tingles through her entire body. From his forearm. As if he was having a similar response to her, he gripped her hand tighter, possibly worried she might run away.

Which was a fairly intuitive reaction, because with every other step she second-guessed her response. What was she doing? She was supposed to be meeting her kids and their significant others for dinner. Not running off with a stranger.

A stranger whose bicep strained the ribbed hem of his short sleeve white Polo shirt. The bright clean white emphasized his darkly tanned, smooth skin. The pique shirt clung to the pectorals and rippled abs beneath the simple cotton. His khaki pants cupped an interesting, mouth-watering bulge. His quads bunched and released beneath the innocuous pants as he strode purposefully toward a small steak house hidden in the corner of the giant lobby.

He wore the uniform of the casually rich, like so many of the men in her home town, but instead of a gym-toned body and slight paunch, he radiated power and a unconscious virility that had her weak in the knees.

Her insides tightened and her sex clenched as she thought about all that power and strength between her thighs. She pictured him above her, his strong jaw tight with determination as he invaded her body with long luxurious thrusts and a fierce sexuality.

She was crazy.

She was imagining sex with a stranger.

A stranger who evoked a pure intense sexual desire that she hadn't felt in a very long time, if ever. She'd been an infant when Jackson Stone Sr. had swept her off her feet.

Now, she was a mature woman.

A mature *horny* woman who hadn't had a man in a long damn time. And she wasn't sure she'd ever had a man that was this much man. He exuded testosterone and radiated a sexual power that would be thrilling and overwhelming in the bedroom. That was still no reason to run away from her commitments and consider doing inappropriate things with a stranger.

Or imagine a man she just met naked and sweaty and rocking her world.

"We'd like a table in the back, if possible." Ric smiled at the young hostess. His teeth were startlingly white in his swarthy face and emphasized his full, dark red lips. One smile and the girl scrambled to make him happy.

Shelley couldn't stop the instinctive eye roll at the girl's obvious reaction to his sensuality. She tried to ease away but he anticipated the move and pulled her closer. So close the heat of his body seeped into hers. Her entire body sizzled as if he exerted some sexual force field that caused the air to whoosh from her lungs and the atmosphere around them to snap and crackle with unfulfilled cravings.

Ric stared into her eyes. "You are so beautiful."

"You're in the land of beautiful." She tried to deflect because really, telling her she was beautiful?—Of course the initial pleasure at a compliment was nice, but—let's get real.

There were beautiful women everywhere in Vegas.

"It shines from inside you, in your bright eyes and the glow of your skin. And it's all the more potent because you don't seem to realize how attractive you are."

With those words, she melted. Because even if it was a line, he'd delivered it with such sincerity that she was loathe to contradict him. She hadn't been complimented like that since Connor when he was in third grade and he'd written a poem about her hair and eyes. Connor! The kids.

She was supposed to be going to dinner with them. Crap. "I need to let my…friends know I won't be joining them for dinner."

"Ah, yeah." He smiled deprecatingly. "Me too."

He moved with an innate grace. He pulled her chair

away from the table in an unconscious move that told her that he was no stranger to the chivalrous gesture. As she sank into the cushioned chair, Ric trailed his fingers across the back of her bared shoulders. What should have been an impersonal touch became a sensual caress as his slightly callused fingers scraped along her nerve endings and shimmered over her skin. Goose bumps peppered over her arms, arrowing from her shoulders down to her neglected sex. Everything tingled.

Shelley needed to focus and settle her family so that she could enjoy this dinner, date, whatever this was.

She sent a quick text to her daughter Jess. *Going to bow out for dinner. See you tomorrow morning at the spa.*

HER PHONE DINGED. Jess: *Everything okay?*

ALL GOOD. *Enjoy your dinner. xo mom*

JESS: *U want me to chk on u?*

No! Panic immobilized her, but she had to play it cool. Otherwise, Jess would be at her door and realize that she wasn't in her room.

SHELLEY QUICKLY TEXTED BACK to her. *All good. Just tired. Love u. mom Turning off my ringer for the nite. Have fun!*

. . .

THE HESITATION that had gripped her earlier was gone. She wanted to be here. Wanted to spend time with this man. Hopefully the promise of him would live up to her expectations. She suddenly knew that she needed this night for herself.

Wanted him for herself.

"Everything okay?" His liquid dark eyes pierced her as if he could see inside her soul to the anticipation that fired her body.

"No problems." She wasn't about to confess that she was texting her adult daughter. This wasn't about getting to know each other, about beginning a relationship, this was about mutual attraction. Mutual satisfaction. Distilled down to its elemental level, this night was about sex.

About him and her in a hot sweaty tangle of limbs and lips.

Bringing up the fact that her daughter was twenty-seven was a sure mood killer. He'd probably dated women younger than Jess.

That quickly, her confidence fizzled again. What was she doing?

"Hey. Where'd you go?"

Shelley pushed back her chair. "Nowhere." She wasn't about to share her mental journey into her sad, lonely history. Before she could stand, he grabbed her chair near her thigh and pulled it under the table. His bicep flexed as he easily moved her back into place.

"Don't go."

"I don't know what I'm doing here," she confessed.

"Having a drink." He smiled, but there was an edge to the smile that caused her pulse to speed and her heart to thunder. "And dinner."

"I don't do this kind of thing."

"Eat?" he inquired with amusement.

"Eat with strange men."

"Hey. I'm hardly strange." His dark eyes glimmered, full of sensual intent, in the flickering candlelight. That focused regard set her off balance again. "But let's change it so that we aren't strangers anymore."

Getting to know each other? Once he knew her, he wouldn't want her.

As if he could sense her jittery need to run, he squeezed her fingers and said softly, "I don't do this either. Not anymore. At the risk of being too honest, at least not in the last five or six years."

Conversely his honesty calmed her. She liked that he waited for her to process his revelation. So she stayed. Settled.

Get to know each other. She could do that. In Monterey, she was the Queen of Small Talk.

"What do you do?" Shelley asked.

He answered, easily, vaguely. "Security."

He didn't hold himself with a military bearing and she should know, since all three of her boys had served. Jack and Riley in the Navy and Con in the Army. He had a casual slouch that in no way diminished his power or intensity. She didn't want to bring up the military.

"How about you?"

There was another conversational topic she wasn't going to touch. Since she spent most of her time in Monterey volunteering, serving on philanthropic boards, and now farming, she tended to forget that she was an extremely wealthy woman.

She didn't get out much, so being a target for a con man or scam artist was usually not a concern. Except since the article in the paper that highlighted her wealth, instead of the ground breaking philanthropic farm she owned, she'd been the focus of several stalkerish emails and internet proposals. Now she was in Las Vegas and Jack seemed to think she needed to be extra careful. He'd warned her before they arrived. Because of the crazies who'd come out of the woodwork after that article, Jack had been concerned for her safety.

"I'm a farmer." Which was true. She had been an avid contributor to the Food for Life food bank for years. And recently she'd bought land and begun a program to work farmland, not for profit, but specifically to supply fresh produce to the local food bank. She was very proud of Happy Tummy Farm. But she didn't want to get into the specifics.

"Ah." Ric still held her fingers in his. He lifted her hand and turned it over so that her palm was open and exposed. Then he kissed the sensitive hollow with a brief press of his firm lips. "That would explain the calluses."

Lightheadedness swamped her.

Good lord, he'd only kissed her palm.

An unexpected moan escaped as he kissed her palm again, his lips lingering. She closed her eyes in a swell of embarrassment so acute she wasn't sure if she'd recover.

"Damn, I want to hear that again." This time he kissed her palm and caressed her with a barely there lick of his tongue against the already sensitized skin.

"Oh my God."

Shelley tried to tug her hand away and squeezed her thighs together as if she could hold in the rush of arousal creaming her exquisite black lace panties.

"*Christos*. I want to hear you moan like that in my ear." He nipped at the heel of her hand and another zing of arousal traveled through her body like a wildfire through a drought-ridden canyon.

Another rush of arousal flooded her. As if an alien had overtaken her body, she placed her hand on his thigh, and beneath her palm his muscles flexed. She leaned over so that her mouth was right next to his ear. Food was forgotten. Getting to know him better was forgotten. All she wanted to was to be alone with him.

"Let's go." Her lips skimmed the whorl of his ear. Her cheek brushed his and though he had obviously shaved earlier, the slightest scruff of stubble scraped against her softer skin.

Common sense reared its head. She needed to be clear. "Only for tonight."

"That works." His hand over hers squeezed tight. He pulled back just enough that an inch separated their noses as he stared into her eyes. His black gaze was like liquid sin. "You sure?"

There it was again. Chivalry.

So she gave him the only answer that she could. "Yes."

CHAPTER 3

$\mathcal{R}$ic followed Shelley into the elevator, admiring her from the backside while the mirrored walls reflected her from all angles. The look on her face was soft, luminous. Her eyelids were heavy and a subtle glow shined her skin.

She had gorgeous lines to her body. She had curves. Not too curvy but enough that no matter where he grabbed he'd have a handful. Which meant she was built for sex.

Dammit. His body was on fucking fire. His erection pressed against the zipper of his rarely worn khakis. He leaned back against the rail and pulled her in front of him, knowing the security guys in the booth just got a great shot of him sporting wood.

Ric slid his hands around her hips and rested his palms on the slightly rounded curve of her belly. The touch was less than sexual but as she relaxed into his embrace, she eased back against his chest.

"Oh." She let out the surprised puff of sound as his dick nestled into the cleft of her ass. He started to try to put space between their bodies but her palms skimmed over his forearms to rest over his hands and effectively held him in place.

Ric nuzzled the sweet spot behind her ear with his nose. "The first time is going to be hard and fast. Is that a problem for you?" He sure as hell hoped not because he wasn't sure he could go slow until he took the edge off this insane lust.

"The first time," she said faintly. But as if his words flipped a switch, she melted further into his embrace.

He ran his tongue down her neck, until he hit her collarbone and then he nipped the thin skin over the delicate frame.

The elevator dinged.

"My floor." One more time he worried she was going to change her mind. Not that he couldn't deal with the extreme hard on himself if need be but he was literally dying to sink into her hot, wet, sex and discover her feminine secrets.

"Thank God." She grabbed his hand and tugged him out of the elevator.

Ric grabbed his key card and shoved the key in the slot, desperate to get inside his room and inside her.

The heavy door swung open and they stumbled in. A soft glow cast light on the side of the bed but the rest of the room was bathed in shadows.

"I need you." As the door slammed shut, Ric shoved Shelley up against the wall and devoured her mouth. He might have felt badly about the rough treatment except she was yanking his Polo from the waist of his pants as he eased down the zipper of her dress.

Her hands were insistent and hot on the skin of his back as she rubbed against the fucking pipe in his pants.

Her shoulders were pressed against the wall but she'd

canted her hips so that the ridge of her pubic bone massaged his erection. He shoved the dress off her shoulders, and it dropped to the carpet.

Ric nipped at her lips as he took in her glory. She was perfect. High pert breasts, a mostly flat stomach with a just a hint of curve, and nicely rounded hips. The see through lace of her bra revealed as much as it concealed, and her nipples speared the delicate fabric broadcasting her arousal.

She wore boy cut, lace panties that matched her bra and a pair of spike-heeled pumps that made her almost as tall as he was.

The sight of Shelley in her sexy lingerie and her heels nearly brought him to his knees. "God damn, you're beautiful."

She ripped his shirt over his head and ran her hands over his stomach. His abs rippled in respond to the scratch of her nails against his six pack. Ric scraped his teeth down the cord of her neck and pressed sucking kisses along her collarbone. "Unbutton." Sucking kiss. "My." Sucking kiss. "Pants."

She caressed his cock through the fabric and he groaned deep and husky in his throat. "Now," he demanded gutturally.

She fumbled with his zipper as he cupped her breast and lifted the globe from the lace so he could suck her distended nipple into his mouth.

Her head thunked the foil-papered wall, while her fingers were busy shoving his pants to the floor. He toed out of his loafers as her hot palm curled around his thick, almost painful, erection.

Her breath caught as she pumped once, twice.

"Dios, *cariña*. Not going to last long."

Ric slid his palms underneath the lace of her panties

and curled his fingers over her ass, shoving the black lace down her toned thighs with impatient urgency.

He wanted nothing more than to push into her tight wet heat. But he'd never gone without a condom and he wasn't about to start now. "Condom," he muttered against her damp skin, his breath made her nipple pucker even harder.

But she still didn't lessen her grip.

"Honey, you've got to let me go."

Once she loosened her hold, Ric paused for a moment to study the picture of her. She leaned languidly against the hotel room wall. Her thick auburn hair tumbled around her shoulders, her breasts popped out of the lace cups, on display for his ardent gaze, and her panties puddled on the floor around her fuck me heels. A simple diamond pendant lay in the valley between her spectacular breasts. Her heavy lidded gaze met his openly and she smiled seductively like a temptress. Her nipples were wet from his mouth. Her legs were slightly apart and arousal glistened on her thighs.

Her heady musk scented the air and ramped him higher, harder.

"Hurry," she whispered.

"Fuck. Don't move." He hustled to the bathroom and thanked God he'd unpacked before he'd gone to the bar. He ripped open the package as he strode back to her, then rolled the rubber over his aching cock.

He was back in a flash, and with one quick eager move he shifted his palms beneath her ass and lifted her up. With a jerky motion he impaled her on his cock.

They both groaned as she sank down, her pussy gripped him tight and to the hilt.

"Wrap your legs around me." She was still wearing the stilettos. Damn if that image didn't make him even harder.

She curled her arms around his shoulders and used her

leg muscles to bounce up and down on his cock. Her heels dug into the flesh of his ass. Ric slanted his mouth over hers and inhaled her as he pounded up into her tight feminine sheath.

Every thrust rubbed the length of his cock against her clit and massaged her. Her breathing became more erratic. With a long lusty moan, she blew over the edge into orgasm. Her pussy convulsed around his cock, sucking, contracting, until he came with a shout, pumping into her with unrestrained fervor. Her breasts bounced with every thrust.

Fireworks exploded beneath his closed eyelids as he pumped and pumped, expelling his come in a burst so forceful his knees dipped and his mind fuzzed at the loss of cognizance. She was digging her nails into his shoulders so hard he'd have marks in the morning and he didn't give a damn.

Her pussy continued to squeeze his erection. Sweat slicked his skin and heat rose from her body. Her nipples rubbed his pecs and her thighs still had a steely grip on his hips as her orgasm seemed to go on forever.

Ric's heart tattooed a frantic rhythm in his chest, banging hard even as the beat slowed. Adrenaline and endorphins pinged through him in a cocktail of sexual satisfaction. God damn, he knew their attraction was off the charts but he still hadn't expected this.

He stayed rooted inside her, as he came down from the intense orgasm.

Ric dropped his forehead to the curve of her neck. His breath heaved in and out as if he'd just finished a grueling PT session. He'd feel bad about attacking her like a pit bull except she'd been right there with him.

Now she was as wrecked as he was. Her thighs went lax and her hands were no longer trying to dig into his flesh, and instead rested lightly on his shoulders, while her back pressed up against the wall.

"Holy shit." He licked her neck, savoring the slightly salty taste. He couldn't wait to taste her in other more intimate places and smiled against her skin. "Told you round one was gonna be fast but, day-um, that likely set the ground speed record for orgasms."

She giggled. The soft sough of her breath over his cheek bathed him with pleasure. He needed to get her in bed and start on round two before she had time to think.

Right now she was flushed and satisfied. A lazy smile curved her lips and her eyes sparkled with a hazy satisfaction. But he was pretty sure that once her brain started firing again she'd try to bolt. And no way was he going to let that happen.

RIC CARRIED her over to the bed. *Carried* her.

A primeval thrill fizzed in her blood. She was in good shape for her age but she was not a lightweight. His biceps bulged as he strode toward the king sized bed but he wasn't struggling at all.

He held her with one arm and yanked the sheets down the bed. Then he knelt on one knee and placed her gently on the cool, high thread count cotton.

She was wrapped around his torso like an octopus. Suddenly she realized that when she let go, he'd be able to see her in all her forty-five year old glory. With her not quite as tight skin, breasts that weren't quite as perky as in her twenties, and the faint ripples of stretch marks on her tummy from Jess. A mother's badge of honor but definitely not sexy.

He started to back away and she held on tight. Fortunately he misinterpreted her tight snug hold. "I'm just going to get more condoms."

Thank God he was prepared. She certainly hadn't planned to have sex when she'd come to Vegas for Jack and Bliss's wedding.

He brushed a lock of hair from her cheek and she forced herself to smile and pretend that she wasn't totally embarrassed about being naked in front of a stranger. As if he understood, his gaze hadn't left her face. He stared at her for another minute, tracing her features, before he headed to the bathroom. The ambient light from the open bathroom door accented the play of his glutes as he moved with unselfconscious grace.

She couldn't help it. She pulled the sheets up and over her breasts. She knew she looked pretty good for her age, but she certainly didn't look anything like the bar bunnies who had been hanging on him earlier tonight.

Her brain started working overtime. What was she doing here? This was madness. She was a mother of four adult children. Even if they weren't all biologically hers. She shouldn't have engaged in a random hook up in a bar.

Her breath shortened. Worry and shame tightened her lungs. Her fingers curled around the sheet as she contemplated throwing it off and making a grab for her clothes.

He tossed three condoms on the nightstand. Three. Condoms.

Her insecurity built. The pressure, the worry that she couldn't give him what he wanted, what she wanted, hit her. And she couldn't draw in precious air.

Then Ric was there. "*Cariña*, take a deep breath."

She realized he was right. She was practically hyperventilating.

He was gorgeous. Lean muscled strength, a smattering of dark hair dusted his pectorals and arrowed down to his hardening erection.

The sight of all that masculinity, the thick purple head of his cock, kissed with a glistening drop of arousal was stunning. His cock bobbed showcasing the V of his muscles, his thighs bunched and flexed as he crawled over her. His body was awe inspiring, but what had her breath slowing and her heartbeat calming, was the intent, intense look in his glittering dark eyes. He wanted *her*.

Why? She had no idea.

"Breathe," he commanded.

He knelt on one knee, curled his palm around her nape and kissed her. His lips were warm and firm. He invaded her mouth with his tongue in a confident, aggressive move.

She loosened her death grip on the sheet and stroked the warm tensile strength of his biceps. She waited for him to lower over her. It was hard to miss what you rarely had but she still trembled in anticipation of his bigger, harder body covering hers. Inside hers.

The musky scent of sex permeated the warm air surrounding them, wrapped them in a sensual blanket of heat and lust. "I can't wait to taste all of you." Her body responded to his words as if he'd licked all those places he couldn't wait to touch.

Ric gently tugged the sheet away from her body. His palm skimmed over the curve of her breast, her nipple hardened into his caress. With a reverent hiss, he trailed his tongue down her neck and then pressed wet open mouthed kisses along her breastbone until he stopped in the valley of her breasts.

His face buried between her breasts was a visual aphrodisiac. His dark hair brushed the sensitized skin of her breastbone and the scruff of his beard was a delicious scrape over her softer skin as he nuzzled one mound with his mouth and cupped the other in his hot palm.

Shelley didn't just want to be a recipient of his sexual attention. She needed to be an active participant in their physical play. She skimmed her toes up the back of his thighs, and gloried in the bunch of his ass beneath her hands. His cock brushed the valley of her stomach like a hot thick brand. Good, gracious, he was hard again, searing her with the promise of ecstasy.

She squeezed her arms around his shoulders trapping his head between her breasts. He snickered and turned his head to the side, licking up the slope before suckling her nipple into his mouth.

"You're not distracting me that easily." He pushed up, disengaging her legs, as he nipped his way down her stomach. She prayed he wouldn't notice the silvery strands of her stretch marks.

But he was too busy tonguing her belly button to comment on her body. Her thighs fell open as he kissed and suckled his way down her body until his nose was buried in the auburn curls at her sex.

He smiled against her clit.

"Oh," she gasped. "You don't have to—"

"You're right." His tongue lapped at her slit in one long languid lick. "I want to."

She'd only had this done to her a few times. And it had been nice but truly she couldn't seem to let go of her inhibitions enough to enjoy it. "Really."

Ric scooped his arms underneath her thighs, lifting her up until the back of her legs rested on his shoulders, his palms cupped her ass, and he was face planted in the heart of her sex. He inhaled slowly, then pressed an open mouthed kiss right over her opening.

He spread his palms wide and pressed down on her lower belly as his tongue continued to do wicked things to her. His swarthy skin was a stark contrast to her pale belly and lighter curls. Her pulse sped up.

"What a gorgeous pink pussy."

Her hips jerked at the dirty talk.

He chuckled against her curls and then used his thumbs to spread her wide. The air was cool against her damp sex. "Someone likes it dirty."

Her entire sex clenched, dying for more of him.

As if he knew exactly what she wanted, he jammed his tongue inside, stabbing in a rhythm that had her clenching wanting more than the bulk of his tongue inside her, wanting the girth and thrust of his cock.

Her feet were planted next to his shoulders and her hips rocked involuntarily into the hot press of his mouth. His slight stubble stimulated nerve endings as her whole attention narrowed to the carnal attention of his tongue and the stroke of his hands.

God it was building again. Her body was like a hot air balloon slowly filling, expanding until she knew she was going to take off in a burst of helium. Anticipating her imminent explosion, Ric's mouth continued to work her sex and he slid his hands up and cupped her breasts.

Then he sucked her clit into his mouth at the same time he pinched her nipples hard. She lifted off, flying as her sex clenched around nothing, convulsing with an explosive fury.

The lusty moan that erupted from her was as much a surprise as her body imploding in a spectacular burst of sexual bliss. She was going to have to rethink her position on oral sex. That had been more than just nice.

She wasn't loud during sex. She wasn't loud anytime. She was proper, and quiet, and dignified. She'd spent years perfecting that persona, dealing with the malicious gossips and their snide comments when she'd first gone to live at the Stone Mansion at twenty-five.

She was a calm placid lake. Nothing could rattle her. And that naturally bled over into her somewhat sparse sex life.

At least it had. Ric continued to work at her, feeding an orgasm that seemed to go on and on and on. "Oh my God," she breathed. "I don't—"

He pulled her closer as she tried to push away from the intensity of her climax. But Ric held her down, pressed on her belly and continue to eat at her. She didn't usually have multiple orgasms. One per night seemed to be her limit so she was already at 200 percent.

She was almost incoherent. "I can't—"

"Of course you can." He smiled, she could feel his lips curving against her sex.

She was forty-five years old and she still had problems with sex talk. It stemmed from early sexual experiences resulting in an unexpected pregnancy. She had stunted her sexual growth. Being a single mother, and then suddenly mother to four at twenty-five, she had skipped the sexual revolution and the world's easy acceptance of casual sexual encounters. Which meant sometimes she had difficulty verbalizing explicit wishes and situations. "But you haven't...."

"I will." He prowled up her body dropping kisses in random spots, her hipbone, the valley between her ribcage, the underside of her breast.

His cock was hard and hot along her thigh. Even as loose as she was right now, taking him again was going to be a challenge. Dammit, if she was going to do this, she was going to do it right.

Her arm was trembling as she reached for the condom packet. "I believe in equal opportunity orgasms. Your turn."

She tore open the package and tossed it onto the carpet. With careful deliberation, she rested the condom on the head of his cock. Her fingers strummed along his thick length. Damn, he was big.

"I'm all for equal rights," he quipped. Ric groaned as she rolled the condom slowly over his erection all the way down to the root.

She explored his body with her hands, running her palms over his broad shoulders and skimming the defined muscles of his lats. With an unexpected urgency, she sucked on his tight nipple and grabbed his ass.

"Trying to slow it down here." Ric panted.

"Why?" she murmured against his mouth. Completely bewildered.

"Mutual satisfaction."

"I've already been satisfied," she said urgently. "Twice."

Ric laughed low and husky, the sound trilling over her nerve endings and stimulating a cascade of shivers. "Yes, you have." He rubbed the head of his cock over her dripping sex. She wanted him inside her again.

Everything in her clenched. She was nearly blind with need. She curled her legs around his butt and urged him to breach her. "Do it." It was a command, and finally he listened.

He slid all the way inside her, filled her up, buried to the hilt, her sex sheathed his girth. "I guess round three will be the slow and steady one."

Round *three?*

But before she could register that thought, Ric began to power in and out of her, and sensation after sensation bombarded her. The heat of his body, the thick invasion of his cock, the rub of his chest hair against her breasts.

Then he tunneled his hands underneath her body and tilted her hips. The new position changed the angle of his thrusts and suddenly the head of his cock rubbed a spot inside her.

Oh my God.

She'd thought the infamous g-spot was a myth. But Ric had just busted that myth wide open.

Shelley moaned. Her channel was on fire as he breeched her body and caressed that sensitive ridge. Her desire swelled and grew in immense waves until she trembled on the verge of another cliff. Impossible.

She never had this many orgasms. But as his body plundered hers, with every rock of his hips, her nerve endings focused on that spot.

His thrusts took on an urgency and he began to slam into her. Each bang increased the pressure on that secret internal ridge, and her body began to shake. He slammed his mouth over hers, their teeth clashed together. Her hips jerked in time to his thrusts as the incredible pressure built, until scent, sound, sensation crescendoed into a violent mind blowing explosion.

Her vision went white, and she clung to his shoulders as if he could anchor her to this world. Ric groaned into her mouth and his body arched back into a rictus of pleasure. His release pulsed inside her. Her body contracted around his as he shot his come into the condom. Her insides fluttered, triggering another mini-orgasm.

Ric was panting as if he'd just run a marathon and she

lay limp and replete beneath him, her body still vibrating with the force of her climax. She couldn't move. She still couldn't believe that she'd come again. "You must be some kind of sex magician. I don't ever…."

He stifled a laugh. "That's me. I'm a regular David Copperfield of orgasms." He was draped over her insensate form. Her arms had fallen to her sides, her legs were splayed open and he was hard and satisfied between them.

He should have been too heavy, instead his weight was comforting, pleasing. He rested his forehead in the curve in her neck.

Shelley snickered. She threaded her fingers through his short hair. "At the risk of…swelling your head—"

"*Christos*, woman, give me a few minutes to recover before you talk about my head swelling again." He wiggled his hips.

She laughed as he'd meant her to do until his still semi-hard cock hit that spot inside her again and she shivered. "I don't ever—"

"Let's change that rhetoric."

"Hmmm?" She was only half listening as she languidly ran her fingers through his hair and over his strong, muscular shoulders. He was really quite beautiful.

He rephrased her former sentence. "I haven't in the past ever—"

"*Fine*," she said emphatically. Too satisfied and sated to be embarrassed. "Ever. Had that many orgasms in one night."

"Let's see if we can set another record." He rolled them over so that she was on top of him. He ab curled up and swirled his tongue around her nipple. Her sex spasmed as his cock pulsed in her overstimulated sheath and his pubic bone rocked against her clit.

"Give me a second." Ric discarded the used condom in a tissue on the bedside table and then ripped open another package.

"Not possible." But good God damn, her body seemed to be on board with another slower round. It was sweet of him but she needed to be honest. "The odds of another orgasm for me are about a billion to one."

"Never tell me the odds."

CHAPTER 4

a loud, frantic pounding on the door woke Ric.

Shelley was draped over his body, one thigh slung over his, her arm across his chest and her chin snuggled into the crook of his neck.

He grinned. Setting records was certainly fun.

The pounding increased in volume. "Jeez. Don't get your cammies in a twist."

Shelley lifted her head sleepily. "Everything okay?" Her rich burnished red hair was a tangled mess around her face, beard burn reddened her chest and neck. Love bites peppered the curve of her shoulder. She looked absolutely wrecked and absolutely gorgeous.

"Probably the maid."

Ric snagged his pants and hustled to the door.

"Come on, BP. Open up!"

Not the maid. He peered out the peephole and sure enough it was his best pal, Jack.

Ric held his pants so he covered his naked cock and opened the door a crack. "Not a good time."

He could hear Shelley rustling behind him. All he

wanted right now was to get rid of Jack and get back to setting more records. He grinned.

"I've been texting and calling for the last hour," Jack snarled.

"Perhaps there's a good reason why I didn't answer," he said mildly. A little surprised since Jack Stone wasn't really prone to outbursts of emotion. He was a cool calculating SOB most of the time.

"Sorry to disturb your love fest." Jack pushed the door open with an irritated shove. Since Ric wasn't expecting it, his body gave instantly as Jack burst into the living room. "I have a big problem. My mom is—"

Jack stopped dead and whirled around. "In your bed? What the fuck, BP?"

"Jack?!" Shelley was clutching the sheet to her chin. She'd drawn her knees to her chest and her eyes were wild as she stared at his friend. But what in the fresh hell was Jack talking about? No way was Shelley old enough to be his mom.

"Shelley." Jack's face was set in a murderous frown as he advanced on Ric. "What is going on here?"

"What?" Ric felt like he'd walked into an alternate universe. His lover from last night couldn't possibly be Jack's stepmother. Could she?

"Well, if you don't know then I guess I need to have the birds and the bees talk with you before you and Bliss get married." Shelley sniped at Jack.

Ric laughed huskily.

Then he frowned when he noted that she had her hand over her eyes and she'd tucked into a ball, making herself a smaller target. Since Jack had burst in here, she hadn't looked at Ric once.

"Jesus, Shelley." Jack looked at such a loss that Ric

wanted to smile but instead he planned to hustle Jack out of here pronto.

"As you can see, she isn't missing. Why don't you give us some privacy?" Ric spread his legs in an uncompromising stance, but his authority was diminished a little by the fact that he was still naked and clutching his pants in front of his dick.

"Jesus, Ric. Put some damn clothes on." Jack said, "We aren't done yet."

Shelley's forehead thunked on her knees. "You're my stepson, not my father." She tried again to lighten the atmosphere but Jack was having none of that.

"So, um, you're Jack's…." Ric gulped. He'd had sex with his friend's stepmother. It sounded dirty, no matter how he looked at it. His gaze snagged on the delicate arch of her collarbone and the hickey on her shoulder and grinned. "You cougar."

Shelley stifled a laugh. He was pretty sure she was smiling beneath her bowed head. "You aren't helping."

Jack muscled his way to stand in between Shelley and Ric. "Put some clothes on. We need to talk."

"I think you've embarrassed Shelley enough for this morning." Ric was suddenly done with Jack's blustering. He knew what kind of man his friend was and he wasn't a saint. Ric and Shelley hadn't done anything wrong, and they were both consenting adults.

Before he could point out that fact—

"And you," Jack turned on Shelley. "Why aren't you answering your phone?"

Shelley lifted her head and stared steadily at Jack. "You really want me to respond to that?"

"Oh for God's sake." Jack rubbed his palms over his

face. "My eyeballs are seared and I may be scarred for life. But I need to talk to you and it can't wait."

"Are all the kids okay?" The panic in Shelley's voice pricked Ric's conscience and that's when he decided to accommodate Jack.

"Sorry, Shel, yes. Everyone is okay." Jack said, "But I need to talk to you. Now."

Ric caught his friend's urgency and unfisted his pants. He pulled them on one leg at a time. The rasp of the zipper was loud in the silent, tense air. Ric grabbed a pair of sweatpants and a white t-shirt from his old Navy duffel. On his way back to the king sized bed he tried unobtrusively to kick the condom package under the overhang before his friend saw the obvious physical evidence of last night's sex fest.

Based on the rigidity of Jack's body, he'd failed.

He handed the concealing clothes to Shelley. "We'll wait in the sitting area while you…." He gestured to the clothes.

He and Jack stepped down from the bedroom area into the expansive living room of the suite and Ric strode over to the massive floor to ceiling windows.

All the Palazzo rooms were suites. He'd upgraded a bit, but the nine hundred plus square feet of space still wasn't enough to make this situation comfortable.

Shelley scooted into the bathroom. He stared at her reflection in the windowed glass, assuming his friend had the decency to not look.

"What the hell, BP?"

Ric crossed his arms over his bare chest and turned around to look his friend in the eye. "How was I supposed to know Shelley was your stepmom?"

He didn't want to mention that they hadn't exchanged a lot of personal details. But he also needed to defend himself from Jack's conclusions. "You neglected to mention that she's gorgeous and she's hot."

"Please stop. I'm going to start bleeding from my ears."

Ric couldn't help but tease Jack a little more. "Did you know—"

"Ric," Shelley said sharply. "Stop."

His lips quirked. He had no grace to be embarrassed. "Come on, babe. You've got to admit, it's a little funny."

Jack turned on the only mother he remembered. "And you."

"There's no Ric on the guest list." Shelley raised her eyebrow. "How was I supposed to know he was your friend?"

"Enrique Santana." Ric extended his hand as if they were just being introduced. "It's a pleasure," he practically purred.

"Cut it out." Shelley flushed and batted his hand away. "Jack, why are you in such a tizzy?"

Suddenly Jack's former animosity fell away. "We couldn't find you and you weren't answering your phone."

There was a solemnness to his face that had Ric sobering up but he couldn't help but defend her. "She's hardly a teenager."

Although she looked like one, swimming in his grey sweats and swallowed up by the large white t-shirt. He couldn't help the primitive satisfaction that he got from seeing her in his clothes with her hair rumpled and her neck reddened from their festivities.

"I told Jess that I'd see her this morning," Shelley replied. "We're not supposed to meet until ten."

"Yeah, but when Jess went to check on you this morning, your door was open."

Shelley frowned. "That's not right. I locked up before I went down to the restaurant."

"That's not all." Jack suddenly looked really reluctant. "Your room had been ransacked. Clothes thrown all over. Your cosmetics were dumped all over the bathroom. Basically your stuff is destroyed."

"What?"

Ric stepped closer to Shelley, his protective urge instinctive.

Jack stared out the window, avoiding his stepmother's regard. "I may have downplayed your threat level."

Ric noticed the shadows underneath his pal's eyes. Something more was going on here than an outraged son. "What threat level?"

"Um, Jack, maybe we should move this discussion to your room." Shelley started backing away from the window, from them. "I'm sure Ric has things to do."

"Not until he answers." A primal urge to protect and defend roared through him. No one messed with his woman.

Wait, his woman? What the hell? One night of spectacular sex aside, he didn't have a woman.

"Really Ric." Oh, the awkwardness here was off the charts. "Thanks for a…lovely evening."

Lovely. Ric wanted to beat his fists on his chest and howl. Lovely didn't come close to describing their explosive encounter.

"We'll get out of your hair."

"No, actually. This is good," Jack said.

"Good?" Shelley had stopped backing away.

Shelley looked like she wanted to bolt again. This time for a different reason. With an inexplicable resolve, he didn't want her to leave.

"What threat level?" Ric asked again.

Jack was glancing between them in pure assessment.

"I'm, ah, fairly well off." Shelley waved away her fortune.

Ric wondered how she'd gotten it. As far as he knew she'd never married Jack's father. Maybe she was independently wealthy.

"When my dad decided to bail on us when I was fourteen, I made some stipulations. Shelley got the house, a small percentage of the business, and full legal adoption of all of us. Dad's only provision was she had to take the Stone name. I think he thought if people believed they were married, women would quit assuming they were going to be the next Mrs. Stone."

Shelley's whole face softened. "Such a fierce protector." Her smile was a little melancholy. "Always looking out for everyone. He was...my champion."

Ric couldn't believe the stab of jealousy that pricked his heart. He didn't want Jack to be her champion, Ric wanted to be the one who put that sweet smile on her lips and that soft look in her eyes.

It was as if her magic pussy had cast some weird emotional spell over him. That random thought had him wanting to take a step back, and usher them out of his room so he could clear his head and go back to enjoying Vegas, all the perks of Vegas, and his friend's wedding.

"Turns out Shelley is a hell of an investor." Jack smiled proudly. Then he bluntly cut to the heart of the problem. "She's loaded."

Coming from Jack that was pretty impressive because although they never discussed it, Ric knew Jack's father was the sole owner of Stone Aeronautic Engineering and that he'd developed and patented some part of a plane that every commercial manufacturer and military contractor used. The guy wasn't just rich, he was mega-rich.

"But how did they find me?" Shelley asked with bewilderment. "I registered under an alias."

Jack paced the living area of the suite, completely ignoring the opulent luxury. "But no one else in the family did. My wedding isn't exactly a state secret."

Shelley snorted. "I was actively involved in the planning. I know exactly how many people know about your wedding." She teased him.

"Even so." Jack said softly, "Somehow they figured out your alias. I really don't like the escalation of this, Shel."

Ric wondered how serious the threat was. "So what's the threat?"

"Really, Ric, there's no need to bother you with this." She made it sound like it was a trivial issue, like having to ration toilet paper in the latrine. But Ric wasn't buying it.

When Jack had been banging on the door he'd been panicked. Now that Ric's head was clearer, he recognized the fear in his friend.

"Shel. BP is in the security business."

"Why do you keep calling him BP?"

"Bulletproof." Jack shook his head. "Damndest thing. He never got shot. Ever."

Shelley made a little 'oh' of distress.

He had plenty of other wounds, but in all his years in the Navy he'd never taken a bullet. Of course, that wasn't relevant right now.

He'd done protection detail on some high level principals. If they needed analysis, he'd make this a working vacation. "I'm happy to help."

"Great. Then it's settled."

"Oh, really, not necessary." Shelley was backing away again.

Rick shook his head. "What's settled?"

"You can be Shelley's protection detail until we figure out where the threat is coming from."

Ric's first instinct was to protest.

"Wait, what?" Shelley beat him to it. "No way."

Perversely, that pissed him off. Wow. "I'm damn good at what I do." He felt compelled to add in a clear, calm voice.

But something in his face must have given him away because she was suddenly contrite. "This has nothing to do with your skills. I imagine you are hyper-efficient, detail-oriented, and highly effective."

Suddenly they were both thinking about his skill and attention to detail in the sack. He could see it in the heat of her gaze.

Shelley closed her eyes, and blew out a breath as her head tilted back on her neck. The angle and clean lines reminded him of a moment last night when she'd been on top of him, riding his cock like a cowgirl, with a look of complete ecstasy on her face and sensual abandon in every line of her body.

His cock responded to the memory like Pavlov's dogs to the damn bell. And he hoped no one was paying attention to his pants otherwise they were going to see the memory response in his morning wood.

"I'm messing this up." Shelley crossed her arms over her chest and rubbed her bare biceps.

She propped her fists on her hips and focused on the extravagant Las Vegas skyline view from his window. It was unseasonably warm this April. Heat shimmered off the pavement, and waiters scurried around the opulent pool delivering food and fruity drinks to the sunbathing guests.

"Only I could have a one night stand who's going to follow me around for the next four days," she muttered.

Suddenly Ric's stomach dropped as he realized he hadn't really taken that into account. Spend the next few days basically glued to her side? That wasn't quite how he'd planned to enjoy his vacation either. Of course, he hadn't planned to have a one night stand that turned into four days of awkward. But he would do it for Jack. And for Shelley.

"And still no one has told me the threat."

"It's pretty nebulous." Shelley blew out a frustrated breath. "You have what belongs to me. I want it back."

Ric touched on obvious points of contention.

"Sounds personal. So did you beat out anyone for a promotion? Or close a deal that forced someone out?"

"I…own the farm outright now. We did have a bit of a dust up last February, but the man involved confessed, it was all hushed up. He received a commuted sentence. Frankly, he's lucky his penalty wasn't worse. I bought him out and the farm is not for profit anyway. I don't have anything of his."

"She's right on that count." Jack nodded. So he was clearly aware of the farm situation.

Ric slipped into work mode. "Are you dating anyone who recently broke off with another woman?" He was thinking out loud. Then he realized what he'd just asked. Obviously they just reached another level of awkward.

"No," Shelley bit out.

He knew it was embarrassing, but really she needed to come clean. "Are you sure? Since this sounds personal. Could they have been dating someone and you didn't realize it?"

"For that scenario to be considered, I would have to have been dating someone."

"Okay well, let's go back a few months. Sometimes these things fester." Ric was thinking about how engaging she was, how funny, how hot, and how sweet. How she could lure away a guy without even trying.

"No one." She ducked her head, and an embarrassed flush covered her cheekbones. Ric smiled at the tumble of her hair.

"Come on, Shel." He cajoled. "I know this is a little awkward but we need to start somewhere."

"Right. Well, my last date was three years ago. I went out to dinner with an older gentleman who was on the Food for Life food bank board with me. He subsequently died a week later. They figured out he had a weak heart." She snapped, "I really doubt his fifty-year-old daughter has hatched some evil plan to come after me."

Ric wanted to laugh at her snarky comeback. But he was stuck on the first part of her confession. "Three *years*?"

She flushed again and crossed her arms protectively over her chest. Ric looked to Jack for confirmation because really, that couldn't be true. No way had the amazingly sexy, hot woman who'd smoked up the sheets with him last night not had a date in three years.

But Jack just nodded.

Three years.

CHAPTER 5

$\mathcal{S}$helley wanted a giant sinkhole to appear in the hotel room suite and swallow her up. The humiliation was almost more than she could take.

She knew she should be upset about the fact that her hotel suite was trashed but seriously it was just stuff. She was more dismayed that her one night stand was now quizzing her about her sex life.

Ric was still standing there, unmoving.

Well, wasn't this special? She'd struck him dumb over her serious lack of sex life.

Now he knew how sexually deprived she was and how much of a total novice she'd been at the whole hook up process. Which would have been fine, if she didn't have to spend the next four days with him shadowing her every move. And explaining her life in excruciating detail.

"That's a great idea," Jack gushed.

Shelley had no idea what idea Jack meant. "What are you talking about?"

"Since I think it's wise not to advertise that you've got a bodyguard, the cover can be that you're dating."

Dating? Oh, hell. That was even worse.

Shelley and Ric winced at the same time. Neither one of them had had any intention of seeing each other again after last night. It was supposed to be a one night hook up and stress free encounter.

Oh my God.

For the first time, ever, she had a one night stand and now Jack wanted him to become her bodyguard. By their nature, one night stands should be anonymous, and over in *one night.*

She shouldn't have to share the embarrassing and scant details of her dating and sex life.

When she was younger and moved into the Stone Mansion, she didn't date. At all. The kids had enough upheaval in their life with a father who was a total man-whore. She'd believed that they needed stability and kept the focus just on them. So, she didn't date when the kids were in the house. By the time she was ready for a date, she'd been thirty-five and had more money than she could ever spend in her lifetime which meant that any interest was slightly suspect. She'd also been unsure about how to go about finding a date.

Now Jack wanted her to 'pretend date' her one night stand.

She wanted to mouth the word, sorry, to Ric. His dark brows were lowered over his deep, secretive eyes while he seemed to be assessing facts.

"It's best if Shelley stays here," Ric said. "I don't think it's safe for her to return to her room."

Jack was nodding complacently as if he hadn't just been chewing her out for spending the night with his friend.

"What?" Stay here. As in stay with him? This just kept getting better and better. "No."

But Ric and Jack didn't acknowledge her growing distress.

Ric shot a guarded look at Jack. His face set in serious lines. "Did you check the room for bugs and cameras?"

Jack said, "Waiting until the cops are gone."

Bugs? Cameras? "You think someone was spying on me?"

"Not necessarily. Maybe they wanted to see your reaction to the destruction." Ric was thinking out loud.

It occurred to Shelley at the same time she saw Ric and Jack exchanged a weighted glance. "It's possible that not going back to your room last night was a good thing."

They'd been waiting for her?

Shelley's heart beat in an uneven rhythm. "So someone could have been watching me? Or waiting for me?"

That tidbit caused her more anxiety than the destruction of her clothes and stuff. The grim looks on both their faces told the story. Her stomach rolled, pitching like she were on a sailboat in the Monterey Bay.

"I have some pics I took before security got to the room." Jack thumbed through pictures taken with his phone to show Ric.

Ric said quietly, "That's an awful lot of rage."

"Let me see." Shelley tried to grab the phone but Jack held it up and over her head. "Jack!"

"It's her life. She needs to see." Ric peeled the phone from Jack's hand. "Besides, she's tough. She can take it."

The off the cuff compliment caused a pleasant tingle in her belly. He casually curled his bare arm around her back, the thick bunch of his bicep was firm and solid behind her shoulder blades while he held the phone so she could see the pictures of her room.

Shelley's breath caught.

But not because of the pictures. Ric's heat seeped through the thin cotton of the t-shirt he'd given her to wear. The memory of her straddling his thighs, her palms pressing on his shoulders, when he'd ab curled to a sitting position and completely rocked her world, had her going wet.

Last night, he had curved one arm around her shoulders and the other low around her hips and guided her as she rode him, his cock splitting her in two, and his arms alternately lifting her up and then slamming her down. They'd bounced so hard the bed had been squeaking and her hair had been flying until he'd taken his fist and gripped her hair to the edge of pain. He had slanted her head so their mouths could meet in a brutal kissing match.

His strength had cocooned her. He had pounded up into her until they came together in a burst of physical ecstasy. His groan had been long and loud against the curve of her breasts as her sex had convulsed, sucking him dry.

It had possibly been the most explosive sexual encounter of her life. She'd clutched his head to her breast and sat in his lap impaled on his cock. He had throbbed inside her, hitting her g-spot and pulsing against her cervix, her ass on his muscular thighs as they flexed and released. Sweat had slicked their skin and sex had smothered the air.

Her heart had been pounding so hard she'd thought she'd pass out from the force of its beats. He'd completely overwhelmed her.

Shelley could feel the flush start in her belly and spread outward like ripples in a pond. She came back to herself, and hoped neither man had figured out where she'd gone mentally.

Super, she was getting turned on. In front of Jack no less.

Right now, Shelley felt protected and safe in the curve of

Ric's arms. She was so much shorter without her heels that she felt almost delicate. Shelley realized she'd yet to breathe, and she made the mistake of looking into his eyes.

The black pools reflected awareness back at her. As if he'd been caught up in the same memory, the skin on his cheeks had tightened and his body hardened. Heat shimmered around them, like a physical wrap of chiffon that made everything go hazy and filmy. For a moment, she thought it was only her being fanciful, until his gaze dropped to her mouth and lingered before his lashes fluttered down over his eyes. She noted the slight beads of sweat on his upper lip, as if he were restraining himself from pushing into her space and claiming her mouth.

God, was it hot in here? All the air sucked from the Universe and her lips buzzed with the reaction to his scorching glance.

Caught in the mesmerizing haze of sexual awareness, she wasn't sure who had leaned closer—her or him or if it was mutual—but the spell was broken by Jack clearing his throat.

"Need my phone back." He reached between them and gently pried the phone from Ric's fingers. "I'll get back to you on any surveillance equipment."

Ric broke their connection, shifting his gaze to Jack. He took a step back from her. And she was momentarily bereft. The air conditioner kicked on and a blast of cool air blew over her, shaking her out of the sexual thrall.

"Good." Ric nodded. "Bring anything salvageable here and then we can discuss an op plan."

Jack seemed unnaturally eager to get out of the hotel room.

But once Jack left the buffer that kept the tension between her and Ric to a low simmer was gone. The silence was fraught, at least on her end, and she started to voice her objection to the arrangement he and Jack had worked out. "I really don't—"

"I know this will be awkward."

That was an understatement. "Ya think?" she snarked.

In the giant sweat pants, soft on her bare bottom and thighs, and the simple cotton t-shirt abrading her nipples, she felt underdressed and out of sorts. She needed the comfort of her own clothes.

Her clothing had become her armor. Her attempt to hide her feelings from the judgment and censure of her neighbors. There were two kinds of wives in Monterey. The old guard who'd been married to their husbands for years, frequently before the men had made their fortunes. And the trophy wives, who'd pushed out wife number one and sometimes number two, to get to those fortunes. The trophies were younger, hotter, and ironically more on edge than wife number one.

Both kinds of wife had something in common. They were always on the lookout for a woman trying to steal their man. Shelley had been a double whammy, she was younger but she wasn't married to Jack Stone Sr. So both sets of wives feared her and shunned her.

Finally she'd found her place, in the philanthropies she supported and the charities she worked tirelessly for, while raising the four Stone children. Over the years she'd developed her armor to shield herself from the venom and jealousy of those wives.

She learned to choose her outfits carefully as a kind of protection from their suspicion, and to guard her feelings from unnecessary hurt.

Without her regular clothing, and clad in Ric's soft

casual sweats, she was stripped of her regular armor and stratospheres outside her comfort zone.

"We're adults," Ric finally replied. "We'll handle it."

Now that Jack had left, the giant elephant in the room, the unmade bed, sat in silent condemnation. The passion from their night was obvious in the absolutely wrecked state of the linens.

Shelley wasn't really familiar with post-one-night-stand procedures. And she wasn't supposed to leave. So what did she do next?

To give her something to do, she leaned over the disheveled bed and tugged on the sheets. She kept her focus on the white linen so that she didn't have to look at him.

She was doing fine with ignoring him until she smoothed the sheet under the pillow and found her lace bra.

The tiny 'oh', that whimper of distress, was loud in the room.

"What's wrong?" Ric asked.

"Nothing." Could this get any more embarrassing?

"As the principal it's your job to tell me if anything is out of the ordinary."

Oh my God.

She gripped her lacy bra in her fist and shook it at him. "Okay. It's out of the ordinary for me to find my freaking bra underneath the pillow in a strange man's hotel room." Shelley's face was as red as the rare steak she hadn't eaten last night by the time she finished. She whirled around so that her back was to him and blinked away tears.

It was too much, the last straw in an emotionally fraught few hours. "That enough intelligence for you?" She shoved back the tears and hoped he couldn't hear them in her voice. Dammit. She hated crying.

God, the temptation to just burrow in the closet and

hide, the way she'd wanted to do all those years ago when she'd first arrived in Monterey, was really powerful. But she was stronger than that. So she did exactly what she'd done twenty years ago.

She put her shoulders back, shoved her chin up, and channeled her inner Eleanor Roosevelt. No one could make you feel inferior without your consent.

She wasn't going to be a victim.

He moved so quietly she hadn't realized that Ric was right behind her until his palms curled over her shoulders. "Hey. Sorry." He turned her around gently and brushed the tears from her cheeks. His voice rumbled from his chest. She stared at his naked torso, amazed all over again that this man had taken her to bed and engaged in hot, sweaty, messy sex with her. But, last night was over, and they needed to move on.

This was going to be awkward enough as it was.

"I'm fine." She shrugged off his embrace and marched over to the puddle of clothing on the floor. She picked up her dress and shook out the wrinkles. She opened the large closet in the bedroom and hung it on one of the heavy wood hangers, then discreetly looked around for her shoes.

The whole time she tidied up the suite, Ric watched her.

Waiting for her to break again? Good luck with that.

"You want breakfast?" he finally asked.

"Sure." She couldn't eat a thing.

He picked up the hotel phone and proceeded to order for both of them. "I'll grab a shower. Do not under any circumstances open the door for any one."

"What about room service?"

"If they come in the next five minutes, which is doubtful, no. Just tell them to leave it outside the door."

She really didn't see what the big deal was. Why would

room service in a hotel this big be a threat? However, she wasn't stupid. If Mr. Security wanted her to not open the door, she wouldn't open the door. "Okay."

He nodded once.

Shelley heard the shower go on, tried not to imagine Ric with water running over his head and down his body, his dark swarthy skin glistening. But the more she tried not to imagine it, the more the images bombarded her. His wide palms and thick fingers rubbing soap over the hair of his chest and following that happy trail down to his groin.

Her flesh heated and her eyes closed on a moan as more images from last night strobed through her. His beard scraping her inner thigh, the iron strength of his biceps as he held her against the wall, the rippled ridges of his abs as he'd pushed inside her.

Sheesh, she was turning herself on just from the memories.

What in the world was happening to her? She considered herself to be slightly asexual. She'd never really needed sex. It was pleasant. A nice release. Clearly something she could live without since it had been a really, really long time.

But last night, he'd awakened something within her.

Like Sleeping Beauty to Prince Charming she'd come alive at his intimate kisses. Shelley snorted. Of course, he was no prince.

He was rough-edged and blunt. So far from her former lovers that the difference was…exciting, thrilling, arousing. The sex had been raw and erotic.

All she could think about was doing it again. With him.

The shower shut off just as someone knocked at the door. Too early to be room service. She wouldn't open it but she could at least go check to see who was there.

She stared out the peephole and her heart sank. With a deep sigh, and only the slightest hesitation, Shelley opened the door. She really didn't want to do this.

"Come on in."

The door swung shut with a solid thunk. Shelley felt more awkward in the borrowed sweats and t-shirt in the heavy silence.

Ric came bounding into the main living area of the hotel room, stark naked, hair dripping wet, and gun in his hand. All those images she had imagined in her head didn't do justice to his absolutely ripped body.

"Shelley, what the hell?" Ric snarled. "I told you not to open the door."

"Mom?" Jess's eyes were wide before she shoved her palm over her eyes.

They stood there in an awkward triangle. Wonderful.

"Ric meet my daughter, Jessica." She dropped down on to the sectional sofa in the living room and threw her arm over her face. "Maybe we should call Colin and Connor and get them over here to see you naked too."

God, the mortification. Was this her payback for failing to mention when they were hot and heavy in the restaurant or banging against the wall that technically she was a mother of four grown adults?

Mary, Mother of— Wasn't she allowed to one thing, one thing, for herself?

"Be right back." Without another word, Ric headed back into the bathroom, presumably to dry off. Shelley was still leaning on the sofa cushions.

"Really mom?" Jess plopped onto the sofa next to her. "I can't decide whether to high five you, because he's hot, or give you a hard time because, Jeez, you're my mother."

She wanted to laugh it off or make some sage comment

because she'd been the one dispensing advice for so many years. But the truth was she was tired. And disappointed. And embarrassed.

Wasn't she allowed to have a sex life?

She wanted to play it off. Laugh, make a joke, be light-hearted and pretend like this wasn't one of the most embarrassing moments of her life, because that is what mothers do. Except she wasn't just a mother. "I'm a woman in the prime of my life." She cursed the fact that her voice broke.

"I know that," Jess's said softly. "It's just a little disconcerting to see what kind of prime you're getting."

Jess giggled.

The sound was so similar to the way she had laughed when she was a little girl that it brought a melancholy smile to Shelley's lips. She'd done a damn fine job of raising her kids. She was proud of that, of them.

"I'm lonely, Jess," she confessed. "You're all grown up and have your own lives now. I just wanted one night…." She trailed off.

"Oh, mama." Jess lay her head on Shelley's shoulder and curved her arm around her waist. "I can imagine."

"Don't imagine too much," Shelley said dryly. "It would scar you for life."

"I love you," her daughter whispered against her shoulder.

"Love you too, punkin'." But she wanted more. Was that wrong?

CHAPTER 6

*R*ic was on his way to talk to security at the hotel. The only reason he'd left Shelley with her daughter was because Jess knew how to fire a gun.

Ric strode down the hallway toward the hotel's security offices. His mind on the break in, but his body itching to get back to Shelley.

Yeah, he knew her daughter had been a sniper and was proficient with firearms, and still, he didn't like Shelley out of his sight.

This low level of panic that streamed through him was unsettling. They had just met.

It was supposed to be a one night hook up, no strings, just some hopefully awesome sex and then *adios*.

Instead he found himself worrying about what was really happening here. He hadn't meant to eavesdrop while he'd been in the bathroom getting dressed, but he had excellent hearing and he'd caught Shelley's forlorn confession when she'd blurted out to her daughter that she was lonely.

Her admission had affected him deep in his gut, because she'd nailed his problem exactly.

That restless, uneasy antsiness that had plagued him over the past year finally had a name. Loneliness.

Maybe it was because in the past he'd spent most of his days with his team, or embroiled in planning and executing ops, but since he'd left the Navy and started his own business, his life had been a series of short term dating partners juggled between jobs.

For the first time in a long time, since his divorce at age twenty, he was interested in pursuing a relationship.

Shelley Stone came with a lot of strings, most specifically four. Three of whom were taller than him and outweighed him by several pounds. But he'd grown up scrapping and scrounging to defend himself and he was pretty sure he could take them in a fight. Individually.

If they ganged up on him, he was a goner.

Even so, he had the strange and overpowering urge to fight for her if they didn't approve. He couldn't believe he was thinking like that.

Focus on the damned problem, Enrique.

Jack had found both listening devices and cameras in Shelley's room. Fairly high tech equipment too. Ric was meeting Jack downstairs in the security offices so they could review the camera footage from Shelley's floor.

Once he was buzzed in to the casino's highly secure offices, Ric beelined for the monitor in the corner where Jack sat with a uniformed security professional.

"What have you got?" Ric hoped they had something to go on.

Jack handed him a stack of photos. "Check out the pictures of her room again. When I went back and looked objectively, something kept niggling at me."

Ric flipped through the pictures. Her clothes were strewn over the floor, looked like they'd maybe been slashed. The cosmetics in the bathroom had been opened and dumped in the sink. Her shoes had been ripped. Ric paused on a particularly pair of sexy red heels and wished they hadn't been destroyed.

His mind arrowed back to last night. Shelley in nothing but her bra and those black patent leather pumps, her legs curled around his ass and her heels digging into him. He'd bet he had bruises on his butt. His lips tilted up.

"Ric," Jack said sharply.

Oops. Ric wiped the smile off his face and studied the pictures again. His first thought when he'd seen the chaos on Jack's phone had been a lot of rage but, after analyzing the larger sized pictures, he had different perspective. "It's a little too…." he struggled for the right word. It was a mess, no question but there was something meticulously ordered about it. "Neat."

"Yeah. That's what I thought too."

The security guy pulled up the video recordings from the prior night.

Jack was clearly uncomfortable. "What time did you guys, uh, meet?"

Ric flushed. "At the bar, about nine." Thankfully, Jack didn't ask what time they'd gotten to his room. Because the land speed record for hook ups hadn't been broken but they'd come close. Their attraction had been that intense.

"Start at 8 p.m." Jack requested the security guard.

They watched the video, scrolling through hours of hotel guests. Several amorous couples; a group of drunk women dressed up for a bachelorette party, the guest of honor wearing a short white veil and a Beauty Contestant banner across her chest that read, "Bride To Be"; one guy with two hookers, one on each arm; and finally at two a.m. a lone man got off the elevator. Before he got to Shelley's room, Ric knew this guy was the one.

He was wearing a ball cap with no logo, long sleeves with a paunchy stomach, baggie Levi jeans, and generic tennis shoes. The cap was pulled far enough down that only his jaw was visible. And he'd angled his head so that no usable shots were captured by the camera.

"No identifying features, tattoos."

Ric eyed the way the guy moved. "Stomach could be fake."

"Yeah. Watch the way he walks. It probably is." Jack studied the man as he paused at Shelley's suite. He didn't look around, no furtive glances or uneasy movements.

"Definitely not an amateur," Ric said which didn't make him feel any better. Then he barked out, "Hold and zoom in on his hands."

Sure enough he was wearing thin latex or vinyl gloves.

"I don't like this," Jack said.

They continued to watch, keeping an eye on the time stamp. "Guy was in and out in under ten minutes."

The man sauntered toward the elevator, no rush, no agitated movements. He displayed no signs of temper at all. At first glance and with the angry words written on her walls, the destruction was an act of rage. However, there was a more calculated intimidation going on here.

"Shift to the cameras in the casino," Ric said. From the time stamp on the floor video, they started watching that elevator on the main floor. But the guy never came out. They knew he had gotten in the elevator going down so they checked each floor's cameras until they found the tape. He'd gotten out on the third floor then walked toward the shops.

Ric's uneasy feeling grew. "We need to talk."

Jack nodded. "Yeah."

"Can you print the best picture of him we can get?" Ric asked the security guy.

The casino ran the image through their facial recognition software but their database was full of known cheaters and grifters, not work for hire guys like this one.

"Sure."

"Print several copies," Ric said.

Jack interjected. "Six."

Ric raised a brow. "Six?"

"Me, you, Con, Riley, Colin and John."

"Who's John?"

"I guess we haven't caught up in a while," Jack said ruefully. "I have another brother."

Seriously? Ric's mind shifted immediately to Shelley. Like she didn't have enough stuff to deal with. "Must have been rough on Shelley."

"Nope. She was the first one to really welcome John into the family." Jack said proudly, "Shelley is one of the most amazing, resourceful, strong women I know."

Ric thought about the woman he'd had sex with last night. She was more than that. She was a sensual, charming, funny, fun woman who deserved a hell of a lot better than she'd gotten lately.

What was he thinking? That he'd be the one to give her what she deserved?

Ric shuddered. It was like her pheromones had wrapped around his brain and squeezed out all his common sense.

They were a hook up, he reminded himself sternly.

A hook up he now had to protect.

"I think the cover of you and Shelley dating will work nicely." Jack interrupted his musings again.

Ric thought of all the things they would do if they were

really dating. His cock started to rise as he imagined he and Shelley exploring this white hot attraction further.

"But Ric." Jack clapped a heavy hand on Ric's shoulder. "One more thing."

"What's that?" Ric asked absently, his mind on all the ways he could 'cover' Shelley.

"No more touching, Shelley." Jack laid down the law.

"What?"

"She's vulnerable." Jack countered. "I don't want her hurt."

"Shouldn't that be her decision?" Ric asked evenly.

"Maybe. But I'm asking you, as a friend, to take care of her, not bone her."

Ric pressed his mouth together. He would try, but he wasn't making any promises. "I understand your position. But Shelley is a grown ass woman. She can make her own decisions. And if she decides she wants me…." Ric thought back to that three years. She'd been right there with him in his hotel room last night. Jack was thinking about Shelley as a mother not as a woman. "I'm not going to refuse."

On the other hand, what the hell was he thinking? One day ago he would have said he wasn't interested in getting involved with anyone, especially someone with lots of strings attached. A relationship with Shelley had strings written all over it. So, yeah, maybe Jack had the right idea.

Not to mention, getting involved with a principal was really a bad idea.

Jack said, "Let me tell you about the notes she's been getting."

Ric help up his palm. "What about Shelley?"

Jack raised a dark brow.

"She needs to be in on this discussion."

"I was trying to protect her."

"You don't need to withhold things from her." Ric pulled out his phone. "Let's all meet in my suite."

"Fine. I'm going to call Con in." Jack studied the picture of Shelley's intruder. "I don't want whoever is behind this to know where Shelley is."

Ric knew Jack would have a better pulse on the situation. "Do you think she's in physical danger?"

"The evidence of the pro would indicate this is more about scaring her, showing her they could get to her whenever and where ever they want." Jack studied the pictures. "And so far the threats have all been fairly innocuous."

A possessive, primitive need to protect her rose in Ric. "They must know enough about her to know you run a security company."

Jack nodded.

"Yet, they still chose to make a move against her." Ric contemplated that fact. "That indicates a level of arrogance that makes me uneasy."

Jack replied, "Maybe they're under the assumption that I wouldn't care if something happened to her."

"Are we sure the threat is really about Shelley?" Ric's gut clenched with an unnamed emotion. Though they'd just met, he didn't want anything to happen to her. "Could it be aimed at you?"

"It's possible." Jack tapped his finger on his lips. "John is investigating a lead on the missing girls. Ava's friends."

"I thought the asshole was awaiting trial."

"He is, but we found a connection to a strip club here in Las Vegas."

"So this could just be to distract you?" Ric thought out loud.

"Except, I'm staying away from John's investigation so

they don't connect it to my family." Jack mused. "At least not right away."

"Then maybe the focus on Shelley is a back end way to get to Stone Consulting."

"It isn't like I haven't made some enemies lately." Jack propped his hand on his hips.

Ric snorted. "Lately?"

CHAPTER 7

There was a knock on the suite door despite the 'Do Not Disturb' placard on the handle.

Shelley sighed and headed for the door.

"Uh, mom. You don't answer the door until this is over." Jess's hand on her arm stopped her. "Let me."

Shelley moped, and shuffled to the sofa. She dropped onto the L-shaped sectional. The sweats which before seemed soft and comfortable now chafed. She wanted her own clothes. She wanted her own life. It hadn't been hers for all of an hour and she was already going stir crazy.

She was used to being busy.

Jess flipped the lock and opened the door. "Come on in."

Shelley shoved into the corner of the large sectional sofa. Her knees were pressed up to her chest and she rested her chin on them as she waited to see who was here now. It felt as if the whole world was going to know that she'd had sex with Ric Santana.

"Hey, Shel." Connor her youngest son and the hardest of all her children to figure out walked in to the living area of the suite. She loved Con. Perhaps more than the other kids. He'd been broken when she'd gone to live in the Stone mansion. Jack Stone Sr. could be a complete bastard. For some reason, he'd been most venomous toward his youngest son.

After Shelley had arrived, she'd tried to act as a buffer. To protect Con from his father's cruel mean streak. She'd never understood why Jack Sr. had such an intensely rancorous response to Connor. He was the sweetest and so intelligent that Shelley had known that he'd surpass her smarts by the time he was a teenager.

"Con." She pushed to her feet and headed for him.

There it was. That slight hesitation, as if he braced himself for her touch, then he wrapped his strong arms around her and she rested her head on his shoulder for just a moment. Sweet, sweet boy. Even if he did still hold himself away from Shelley's affection.

The only person he didn't hold back with was Ava. His girlfriend.

"Jack asked me to meet you guys here but I'm not sure—"

The hotel room swung open. Jack and Ric strode into the room and over to where Shelley, Jess, and Con stood.

Shelley noted Ric's glare at her until he shifted his gaze to Con and it lightened. What did she do now? She'd tried to get out of his hair. He'd been the one who insisted that she stay in his room.

"Con, there's some leftover breakfast if you want it." She reverted to mom mode, trying to take care of everyone, feed everyone.

"Why are you eating breakfast in Jack's former CO's suite?" Con frowned.

Shelley flushed.

Jess whispered something in Con's ear and his eyebrows rose.

Wonderful. Maybe Ric would like to strip naked so Con could see him in the buff.

Shelley turned her glare on Ric.

He raised his dark eyebrows and held up his palms in surrender. His face was perfectly impassive but she could tell that inside he was laughing. She wasn't sure how but she could tell.

"Quit laughing," she hissed at him.

Ric blinked as if surprised. It was clear that she had shocked him by recognizing what was going on behind his blank face.

"Nice to see you again Connor," Ric said blandly.

"I'm going to head downstairs and pick up some new clothes for you." Jess hugged her tight.

Thank Goodness. "Yes, please."

Shelley flushed again when Con said, "You don't have anything to wear?"

Jack diverted Connor's attention. "Shel, we've got some pictures to show you."

They all sat on the sectional sofa. Jack on one side and Con on the other. Isolation surrounded her, separating her from her family and whoever was stalking her. Then Ric sank down on the glass topped coffee table directly across from her. His thighs bracketed her legs, heat rose from his body. His worn jeans and the body hugging gray Polo shirt were casual, without any attempt to make a statement. The kind of clothing a man supremely comfortable in his own skin wore.

His subtle air of command wrapped around her, making her feel as if nothing could penetrate his shield of protection.

Her tension wound tighter than Ric's abs as he handed her a picture.

The quality was decent, but the man had tilted his head at such an angle that she couldn't see more than his jaw line. The baseball cap brim, a generic denim material, covered most of his face. The angle of the camera made it impossible to figure out how tall he was.

But she recognized the entrance to her suite.

"That's the guy?" Her heart thumped.

"Yeah," Jack said gruffly. "You recognize him?"

Shelley tried to study the man objectively, searching for some clue to his identity but too much was hidden by the way he avoided the cameras. "No."

This man had gone into her room, cut up her clothes, dumped out her cosmetics, and violated her stuff.

It was just stuff.

But what if she'd been in that room?

Sweat bloomed on her chest as the destruction of her room came back to her. He'd sliced her clothes. If she'd been there would he have sliced her? Her heart picked up the pace as horrible possibilities flashed through her mind. Her breath shortened and her finger trembled as she traced it over the man's face.

"I don't even know him," Shelley whispered. "Why would he hate me so much he'd destroy my things?"

Ric's knees touched hers. "Hey. You weren't there." He rested his elbows on his knees and leaned in to smooth his palm over her forearm and linked his fingers with hers. "I won't let anything happen to you."

His touch soothed her immediately.

Shelley lifted her gaze from the picture. His dark, brooding eyes were sincere and she fell into the bottomless promise of safety. She wanted to respond to his pledge. The solemn words felt like more.

Not just here and now. But weighty as if she could depend on him forever.

Instead of making her run, fast and far, she leaned closer until they were only inches apart. "Okay." The air was heavy with expectation.

Con tapped the picture, breaking the connection that thickened the air around them. Shelley and Ric leaned away from each other at his interruption.

"We're pretty sure that this was only meant to scare you." Jack's voice was gentle.

"They did a good job of scaring everyone." Shelley's sense of humor rose again.

"How so?" Con asked.

"There are three of you in Ric's suite, and you're all hovering." Her lips quirked, and she tried to find the humor in the situation. It was either that or curl into a fetal ball and retreat from the world.

"Good point." Jack's lips quirked. "But the fact is that if you look at the mess he made it's too neat, too methodical. Initially we thought rage, but after looking at the larger pictures, we think this was supposed to be intimidation."

"So what do you think they want?"

"They want you to leave," Ric said. The message had been sprayed over the walls. *Leave or else*

Shelley's ire rose. "No. Not happening. I am not missing your wedding," she vowed to Jack fiercely.

"Okay." Con popped open his laptop. "We need to go over the other threats you've gotten."

"It's just a few random emails." Shelley dismissed the weird letters and proposals she'd been receiving. Really, there wasn't anything in those fishing communications that was truly threatening.

"That's my specialty." Con smiled, the action softened the skin around his eyes. He was so much more relaxed and happy with Ava in his life. "I trace things."

"You know, sometimes I think we should thank Fernandez," Shelley said softly to him.

Con lifted his inquisitive gaze from the screen to her. "What?"

"He brought you and Ava together."

Prior to his relationship with Ava he'd still had traces of that defensive teen. Con had needed someone just for him. And he'd found her in Ava. He deserved the bone deep happiness that bled from his pores and bathed him in a soft content light. Shelley brushed her fingers over the lock blond of hair that always seemed to tumble into his tawny eyes.

"True." Con hesitated, then curled his fingers around hers and held her hand for a moment. The unconsciously affectionate gesture rolled over her like a wave of joy for his happiness, and his ability to finally settle in his own skin. "Was there a reason you brought up Fernandez? You think he has something to do with your current problem?"

"Don't knock intuition." Jack stared at the computer screen.

"Fernandez." Ric frowned. Oddly, his gaze was on Con's hand on hers. "Shelley didn't have anything to do with taking him down."

"Not really."

Con launched into a quick rundown of the situation with Jose Fernandez, the politician from Monterey who had used a horrific kidnapping of four young Hispanic girls to advance his career. "We exposed him for the fraud he was.

But you're right, Shelley wasn't really involved, with the exception of giving Ava a place to hide until we were ready to confront him."

"True." Shelley smiled reminiscently.

"He could be attempting to get to you and Jack through Shelley," Ric mused. "Does he know how close you all are?"

"Everyone knows how close we are, ever since that article about the farm—"

"What article?" Ric clipped out.

"It should have been nothing." She hated the attention on her. "The article was supposed to be about the program we, I, implemented. A new kind of way to support the Food for Life food bank. Supporters sponsor an acre of land. The cooperative farm grows the food. Then the harvest goes straight to the food bank so that the recipients have access to fresh produce."

"Instead, the reporter profiled Mom," Jack said.

"I knew having my picture taken in front of the house was a mistake." Shelley shook her head. She'd tried to finger comb the tangled mess of her hair but it was still untidy around her face, distracting her from their serious discussion. She couldn't control the shiver as she remembered how it became so messy. Ric's hand fisted in her hair, holding her head tightly. Like he'd never let her go. Her body reacted to the visceral erotic memory, zooming her right back to that moment in bed.

"The end result was still an increase in people willing to adopt an acre of land and a big boost for Happy Tummy Farm and the food bank, but it also brought attention to me personally. I've gotten several proposals and, um, offers."

"Proposals?" Ric said slowly.

"Um, yes, marriage proposals." Shelley shuddered. "From strangers."

It had been so weird to be the focus of that much attention. She tended to stay in the shadows. She supported plenty of causes but quietly behind the scenes. She'd learned long ago that having money meant many people wanted you to part with it. She'd finally had to pick a few philanthropic efforts, get involved in the process, and choose those projects that spoke to her.

Ric's lips quirked.

"Laugh all you want but having a stranger show up on your front lawn with a marquee and marching band to ask for your hand in marriage is a little disconcerting."

The attention made her uncomfortable.

Even the regard of the three other people in this room made her squirm. She was much better at lavishing attention on the kids, or her charities, than taking it for herself.

"Okay." Ric was suddenly all business as if he sensed her need to fade into the background.

Con pulled up her email account.

Her email. "How'd you do that?"

He just looked steadily at her. "This is what I do, Shel."

"Invade privacy?" Indignation rose in her. First her hotel room, now Con was invading her personal email. "How'd you get my password?"

"We need to have a talk about your password,"
Con said.

Shelley's face burned. She knew it was dumb but that date changed her life. The day she'd gone to the live at the Stone mansion. And it was too personal to share with Ric Santana even if they had shared bodily fluids. "Not now."

Ric got them back on track. "Show me the emails."

She pulled them up. She wasn't sure she should tell him. "I deleted the ones that were um, more personal."

"Personal how?" Ric was back in her space, his chest puffed and his body somehow bigger. He'd morphed into Mr. Protection.

"More proposals offering to…satisfy me."

"How many exactly?" Ric pressed.

"I didn't count. I just deleted."

"Con?" Jack prompted.

"On it." Connor's fingers flew over the keys and within about a minute he had an answer. "Around one hundred."

"A hundred? Seriously." Ric's eyebrows raised in surprise.

"It's that surprising?" She hopped up and strode to the windows, focusing on the skyline instead of her currently complicated life. She curled her toes into the plush carpet and tried to ground herself. She was spiraling out of control and she couldn't seem to stop it from happening. "I'm not dog meat."

"Shel," Ric's voice softened. He approached her, his reflection in the glass was concerned. He cupped his palms over her shoulders. "Of course not. Tactically, I'm trying to figure out how many people we have to investigate."

The heat from his hands burned through the thin t-shirt. She was out of sorts and out of control and she hated it. "This is so crazy."

"One step at a time." Ric tugged her so that her back pressed against his front and his arms wrapped around her tightly. "We'll figure it out."

Accepting his help felt strange. She looked out for herself. She had since she was eighteen and pregnant, her mother kicked her out of the house, and Jackson Stone shoved money at her for an abortion.

"Let's get back to the heart of the matter." Jack glared at

the way Ric was touching her, staring intently at the contact of Ric's hands on her shoulders.

Ric lifted his hands off.

"Well, I would think you should start with the people who asked me for money," Shel said reluctantly.

She thought about the other words on her hotel room wall. *You have what's mine, I want it back.* Although how her money was theirs, she had no idea.

"How many of those are there?" Ric turned her around so that she could looked into his gaze. Without her shoes on, their height discrepancy was far more pronounced. His larger broader frame dwarfed her but the effect was comforting rather than menacing.

"Can't say as I counted." She snarked.

Jack cleared his throat. "I've got the full list."

Her eyebrows rose. "The full list?" Her voice got softer.

"I started intercepting the emails and diverting them into a separate follow up account." Jack said, "You didn't need to see all that crap."

"I can handle my own life."

"Sounds like it's more than any one person could handle." Ric diffused the tension that blossomed between her and her two sons.

"We were just trying to take care of you, Shel," Con said. "The way you took care of us."

With his words, everything in her softened. She loved her kids. "I really can take care of myself, sweetie. Been doing it for years." But the their intention was sweet.

"Now it's time to let us help you." Ric turned on his charm, the same charm that convinced her to go with a stranger to his hotel room. But thinking about it now, she'd made that decision without all the facts. What if Ric had been one of the crazies that had been dogging her life for the past few months?

Ric's gaze had darkened. He was thinking the same thing.

"Connor, your job is to track the emails," Ric directed then he turned to her. "Any other people who physically invaded your space?"

Tension sloshed in her stomach, making her realize she hadn't eaten much of the breakfast and she hadn't had dinner last night.

Shelley shared the details of the people who had actually approached her in person. "But none of those people seemed intent on harming me."

They discussed the logistics of getting to the bottom of the mystery.

"So we're all on the same page here." Ric seemed to have taken over. "Jack, you need to keep working on that other thing. Con, keep at the computer investigations."

While they were discussing the details of her stalker—how weird was that?—things were easy to overlook. But as the conversation wound down and everyone had their assignments, Ric said, "I'll be in charge of physical protection detail."

The reality that she was essentially stuck with Ric Santana, the man who was supposed to be nothing more than a one night stand, hit her again.

A knock on the door had all three men reaching for weapons.

Ric peered through the peep hole. "It's Jess." He stowed his weapon in the holster at his waist, and unlocked the door.

Jess breezed in with several shopping bags. "Got you set up."

"Thanks, Jessy." Shelley hugged her daughter tightly.

"Let's connect again in a few hours," Ric said. He looked around, "By the way, where is Riley?"

"He and Di are on their way back from the Philippines." Jack said, "They'll be here in a few days. But I already gave Ry a heads up."

"I'm just going to put on some fresh clothes." Shelley flushed. Awesome. No one had been paying attention until she brought up the fact that she was wearing Ric's clothes.

As if she sensed her mother's discomfort, Jess said, "I'll be along in an hour to get you."

Ric barked. "I don't want you going anywhere without me."

"Spa day," Shelley said brightly, trying to distract everyone from the fact that his immediate response had been over the top proprietary. Even if he was supposed to be protecting her, there had been an extremely unprofessional note in his voice.

"I'm going with you."

Jack and Ric exchanged another weighted glance. Ric nodded at Jack.

"I'm out," Jack said.

"See you later mom." Jess headed for the door.

"Keep her safe," Jack commanded Ric.

Con gave a chin lift to Jack and Jess. "I'll be along in a minute."

CHAPTER 8

*C*onnor Stone was a wildcard, a little out of step with his brothers. Ric could predict Jack and Riley's response to a situation but Connor played his hand close to the vest.

This was going to be interesting.

Ric waited.

Shelley had already made a dash for the bathroom. She disappeared to put on the new clothes that Jess had brought up from a boutique in the massive mall attached to the Palazzo and Venetian.

Con stood at parade rest, hands clasped in front of him, body relaxed yet ready. "I'd like to ask your intentions."

Ric blinked. "My…intentions."

"Yes, sir."

He hesitated. His intentions last night had been to engage in hot, anonymous sex with a sultry woman. But he didn't think that's what Connor wanted to hear and he wouldn't embarrass Shelley by revealing the truth of their encounter.

"Shelley is an adult," Ric said evenly not answering the question.

Connor shifted closer, his gaze intent, narrowed. "Who, for all intents and purposes, has had very few adult relationships. She's…special."

Ric knew that. He appreciated Con's defense of his stepmother. He did. Although he felt about fifteen and standing in his girlfriend's living room while her father glared at him accusingly. Ric nodded but again didn't say a word.

"Okay. I'll be watching you."

Ric was waiting for Connor to point his fingers at his eyes and then back at Ric like some kind of overlord.

Connor warned him. "Don't hurt her."

The inference that Ric would hurt Shelley pissed him off. "I'd rather have you trying to find whoever trashed her hotel room." Ric couldn't help but needle him.

"That's next."

Connor bulked his shoulders and clenched his fists, and Ric relented. "Connor. I don't want anything to happen to her either. I'll do my best."

"It damn well better be the best you've ever done." Con bit out, "Don't fuck up."

His fierce protection of Shelley made Ric respect him more. "I won't let anything hurt her."

The door to the bathroom opened just in time. Shelley stepped into the bedroom. She glanced between Ric and Con. "Everything okay here?"

Con nodded. "I'm going to get started tracing these people."

Shelley smiled. "Thanks, Con. I hate to ruin everyone's vacation."

"You aren't ruining anything," Ric refuted. "And don't worry. We're on it."

Con bent to brush a kiss over Shelley's forehead. Ric observed the slight hesitation before he touched Shelley. "Stay aware of your surroundings at all times. And…listen to Ric, he knows what he's doing."

Vindication, of a sort.

"Okay, sweetie."

After one final, brusque nod, Con strode from the room. Ric couldn't help but be thankful that her kids were taking the threat seriously.

They were alone. The nine hundred and forty square foot hotel room suite that had seemed so spacious when half of her family had been in the room, suddenly shrunk. The sexual tension that had dissipated with everyone here blasted back into his mind as he registered her outfit.

Black yoga pants, a gift from the Gods, hugged her spectacular ass and thighs, and the deep pink clingy spandex jacket with its mock turtleneck and short zipper clung to her small high breasts. Ric flashbacked to last night, lifting her to his mouth and savoring the sweet taste of her surrender.

Inappropriate thoughts swirled through his mind, promises he'd made to Jack, promises to Connor, and more importantly, to Shelley. He wasn't about to let anything happen to her.

That meant keeping his distance. She wasn't a hot pickup anymore, she was his principal. And getting involved with a client was the worst possible decision in a protection scenario. No touching, he repeated silently, no touching.

He was on board with that mantra right up until she shuddered. Shelley wrapped her arms around her waist and closed her eyes.

"Hey, hey." He couldn't ignore her worry and there was

no one else here to comfort her. Ric tentatively pulled her into his arms. As if his touch unleashed her restraint, she launched herself into his arms her body shaking. She tucked her head into the crook of his neck.

"Don't cry." He couldn't deal with a crying woman.

"Cry?" She shoved out of his embrace. "I'm not crying. I'm pissed."

Relief poured through him. Oh, thank God.

"Someone is messing with my family. My kids deserve a worry free, relaxing vacation. You know this is the first time we've taken a family vacation in years."

She stomped around his room, her eyes bright with indignation. "Jack and Bliss deserve the week before their wedding to be happy and stress free. They've already endured so much."

Ric opened his mouth to agree.

"And Con! He and Ava went from being a couple to having Maria live with them. Helping her adjust to living in the real world again. They have their own hotel room so they can finally have some much deserved privacy. They don't need to be dealing with this crap."

Ric figured Con managed to get some private time with his girlfriend but before he could bring that up, Shelley waved her hands in the air. "Jess and Colin are adjusting to working for Jack. And Colin moving here to the US, to another freaking country for Pete's sake. And Riley and Di have been running as many school supplies as they can to the Philippines since last November. If they're not delivering supplies, they're fundraising and banging on doors getting donations. They deserve to enjoy this time. Not be bothered by nutjobs and have their vacation ruined by some crazy person."

Ric noted in that long-winded diatribe that not once had she mentioned herself. "And you Shelley."

"What about me?" she asked crossly.

"What do you deserve?"

She opened her mouth, closed it. Then frowned. "What?"

"You mentioned everyone in your family except you. Don't you deserve a nice, drama free vacation and celebration of Jack's wedding?"

She shrugged, and the action drew his gaze to her breasts. Her beaded nipples poked the silky fabric, sharp little points in a room that was far too warm for those tight berries to be a response to cold. "Sure."

He could tell she didn't believe that she was entitled to the same things. Her disregard for her own happiness made Ric want to give her everything she deserved and more.

So much for his easy and uncomplicated vacation. Fuck it. He realized he didn't like easy or uncomplicated anyway. He tucked the multi-colored red and brown strands of her hair behind the shell of her ear then trailed his fingers along her neck. She shivered from the light contact.

"You're so fucking responsive," he murmured.

The air thickened with the swirl of pheromones. Shelley caught her breath. His body responded to the subtle signals she was emitting. The softened posture, the prick of her nipples against her top, the languid droop to her eyelids, as he eased his finger beneath the stretchy knit neckline.

Her pulse thudded in the hollow of her throat and the urge to run his tongue along the same path his finger had taken was overwhelming.

His blood rushed in his ears, drowning out everything but the sound of her breath. He was so attuned to her that he could hear the deep thump of her heart against her breastbone. Her feminine scent, floral and sandalwood entwined, flooded his awareness. His cock rose as heated intimate moments from last night swirled in his mind. He cupped her jaw in his hands, his fingers threaded through her hair to hold her tight, or hold her up, he wasn't sure which.

Ric bent his knees and pressed his lips to her thudding pulse. Her skin was satin smooth beneath the purse of his mouth. He couldn't resist the temptation. He swirled his tongue over the sweet evidence of her desire.

Shelley gripped his wrists, holding on to him tenaciously. He groaned against her throat as she leaned into him.

His lips moved over her soft skin. "We need to stop." But damn he didn't want to stop. He wanted to drown in her. Drown in her exquisite taste, drown in her honest sexual reaction, drown while she took him under in a wave of lust so primal his body sizzled with the urge to submerse in her.

Shelley skimmed her palms along his forearms, then his shoulders until she buried her fingers in his hair and fisted her hands. She scraped her lips along his stubbled jaw, and nipped at his ear lobe.

She rubbed her rounded tummy along the weapon in his jeans. She got him so hot so fast, it was as if he'd time traveled back to his teens.

He knew they needed to stop. Before they left this hotel room, he had to get his badass, stalker kicking vibe back because he could do no less for this amazing woman. He had promised to protect her. He couldn't do that if his head was wrapped up in making love to her, not watching her six.

Ric held her in place against the wall, and traced a path from the curve of her collarbone up her neck and along her jaw until he returned to her lips. He pressed gentle sipping kisses to her mouth. His lips clung to hers with each longer inhale, until he finally pulled away.

Ric rested his forehead against hers, eyes closed, and he savored the press of her breasts against his pecs. "I need to be focused."

She laughed, a small puff of breath. "You seemed awfully focused a second ago."

He smiled. "Wrong focus. I need to stay focused on your protection. But, later, after this is over, I'd like to shift the emphasis to…more intimate endeavors."

That was breaking the rules of a one night stand.

She tensed a little in his hold. Shit, maybe he'd misread her enthusiasm.

"I know it's violating the unspoken laws of a typical one night stand," he spoke quickly before she could shoot him down.

"We're so far past typical that we might as well give up and call this thing something else." Shelley squeezed his shoulders. "I'd like that as well."

Ric's tension eased. They were on the same page.

Her face darkened, a crinkle crimped the skin between her brows. "I don't understand why someone one would want to scare me."

"You're gorgeous, nice, and rich." Ric stated the obvious. "You have it all."

"I have a wonderful family that matters and a big house. But I definitely don't have it all." Shelley thunked her head on the wall.

"But to the outsider your life is perfect." Ric smoothed her hair away from face. She had to know that to the casual observer her life was idyllic.

"Yeah, if they only understood how lonely I am." She visibly shook off her melancholy. "Oh shut up, Shel."

She brushed her palms down her sleeves like she was brushing off the attitude.

"Poor little me," she said viciously.

"Hey." Ric said, "Don't be too hard on yourself. It's okay to want more."

"I just want to make a difference," she said firmly.

He noticed she didn't say she wanted more for herself. Every time she spoke up and out, it was for someone other than herself.

"Why the food bank?" Ric asked suddenly.

"It's a worthy cause."

"It's an excellent cause." Ric felt like he already knew her better than that. She didn't just do things because they were worthy causes. He'd skimmed the article that seemed to jump start the crazies who were hounding her and stalking her but he hadn't seen a mention of the impetus behind that particular charity, so he asked again, "Why the food bank?"

"You ever have to choose between a place to sleep and a meal in your stomach?" she asked abruptly.

"Fortunately, no."

She nodded, her burnished red hair skimmed the curve of her shoulder. "It sucks."

So she was saying that she….

"The reason I went to Jack Stone Sr. years ago was because I was tired of worrying about Jess being hungry." She said softly, "I wasn't planning on staying at his house. I tracked him down to ask for a job so Jess and I could eat."

Ric's stomach cramped at her matter of fact statement. He knew it was twenty years ago, but he could tell that the moment still rankled.

She laughed bitterly. "Jack Sr. is a bit of a prick in case you weren't aware."

"I've heard." Jack hadn't said much about his father, but the little he'd shared was enough to give Ric a fairly clear picture of the bastard. "What happened?"

"I got there. And Con opened the front door." Shelley had a faraway look in her ocean green eyes. "He was like a little wounded angel. Their latest nanny had just quit. Literally."

"As in literally?"

"She thought she was going to be the next Mrs. Stone." Shelley shook her head. "As if anyone who knew Jackson would want that. I wouldn't wish him on my worst enemy."

"I must have caught Jackson at just the right moment. He was headed out of town with no one to watch the kids."

"So he asked you to stay?"

"Initially he offered me a lump sum to leave Jess and never come back."

"Holy hell."

"It had worked with Connor's mother." Shelley shrugged. "I can't imagine."

"You turned him down?"

"I didn't want his money. I just wanted a safe place to sleep and enough to feed my daughter. So I suggested I take care of all of his kids instead." Shelley smiled. "My desperation led to the best things that ever happened to me."

Ric's heart expanded. She was magnificent.

"I love all of those kids as if they were my own," Shelley said.

"You know it's mutual." Ric couldn't help but reassure her.

"I know." Tears shimmered in her eyes. "We need to find this asshole."

"I will." Ric vowed. Her sadness made him want to take

away her pain and make her laugh. "Besides now I have extra incentive."

"What's that?"

"The sooner I find this fucker, the sooner we can go back to bed."

And just like he wanted, she laughed.

CHAPTER 9

The phone rang.

Ric held up one finger and stalked to the bedside table. "Santana."

To keep her mind off her other troubles, Shelley admired the play of his glutes beneath his jeans. His short shirt sleeves accented the muscled strength of his forearms.

That quickly she was in that moment last night when he lifted her up against the wall and pushed inside her.

Shelley's knees went weak and her head light.

All that leashed power and testosterone had coalesced into the hottest sexual encounter of her life. Of course that wasn't saying much since her prior encounters had been fairly tame. But a hundred times yes, she wanted to try again.

Because what if her off the chart response wasn't a fluke? Or a lack of response to sexual stimulus over the past few years? And instead their mutual detonation was an honest to God, organic reaction to their chemistry.

After several uh huhs, he hung up the phone.

"Everything okay?"

The panic on his face was priceless. "Spa time."

She giggled when he grimaced. "Think you can handle it, tough guy?"

"Not a problem," he replied smoothly. "But you follow orders. Without question."

Ric opened the hotel room door, held up his palm and re-conned the hallway before gesturing to Shelley that it was safe to come out. "Tell me what's planned."

"Full day. Yoga, massages, facials, lunch, and the hydro-spa." She wasn't sure but he may have just shuddered.

Ric walked in front of her and slightly to the right, his hand resting on the grip of his weapon.

A little shiver of fear ran over her. "Isn't the gun overkill?" After all, the man had only trashed her hotel room.

"I take your safety very seriously." Ric pressed the button for the service elevator. "Behind me, out of sight when the doors open."

She swallowed, licked her lips. "What about your safety?"

"Not important, as long as you're safe."

"I don't like that." Shelley's stomach roiled at the thought that Ric could get hurt because of her. "At all."

"Your feelings are insignificant."

"Nice."

"Shelley. We can't have this discussion now." Ric led her in to the service elevator that the staff used. "I don't like this."

They were on the fifteenth floor. Their choices were the service elevator or the stairwell. Neither was optimal. They rode the elevator to the third floor in silence. Ric pushed her behind him again, the heat from his body surrounded her, reminding her that he was putting himself in front of her.

She hated that.

"Maybe we should re-think this. I don't want you to get hurt." The doors slid open. Ric finished perusing the hallway and let Shelley exit the elevator.

"It would be more than fine with me if you want to go back up to the room where I know you'll be safe." Ric constantly scanned the hallway as they headed toward the spa. "However, don't worry about me."

Shelley bit her lip. "I don't want to let Bliss down."

"Then, in you go."

Bliss, Jess, and Ava waited in the lobby of the Canyon Ranch SpaClub. Instrumental flute music and tinkling water fixtures were supposed be soothing to the ear but Shelley was so tense she wasn't sure anything was going to calm her. The atmosphere was distinctly feminine, which only emphasized Ric's stark masculinity.

Shelley introduced Ric to Ava. He nodded to Jess and Bliss, who he'd met in DC with Jack earlier in the year.

Their party was a melting pot of pretty. Bliss was half-Irish, half-Chinese with bright red hair and exotically tilted eyes. Ava was gorgeous with long dark hair and her beautiful dark eyes. And finally Jess with her multi-hued blonde hair and cool green eyes.

The receptionist was frowning at Ric. "He can't come in unless he has an access pass."

Ric opened his mouth to argue but before he could say a word, Shelley leaned over the desk. "Add it to my account."

"Did you book the appointments under your name?" Ric drummed his fingertips on the check-in counter.

Shelley blinked. "Umm, yes."

"That is a security issue." He glanced around the reception area, empty except for their party. "I don't like it."

Shelley put her hand on his forearm. His muscles flexed

beneath her fingertips, the zap of electricity took her off guard. As if he had a direct line to her erogenous zones, Shelley's body heated, softened.

"This is Bliss's bachelorette day." Shelley didn't want anything to ruin Bliss's party. "Please."

Ric calculated options for another moment. "Okay. But I need to stay with you."

She wasn't used to having a bodyguard. Having Ric around constantly was going to be unsettling and unnerving, but if that's what it took to make sure Bliss had her special day, then Shelley would do it.

"Thank you." She wanted to lean up and kiss his cheek but instead she stepped back and smiled with gratitude.

His dark gaze followed her movements and somehow she thought perhaps he had known what she wanted to do. His gaze dropped to her mouth, lingered there, before sliding to hers.

Ric's tone was all business. "You're welcome. You do what I say, when I say it, no arguments."

Shelley nodded.

"Hannah will show you to the changing rooms." The receptionist smiled tightly clearly not happy with Ric's presence.

The girls changed into their yoga gear. Shelley and Ric waited tensely in the private exercise room that was meant to be calming with its bamboo papered walls, a fountain trickling in the corner, and rolled yoga mats sticking out of a large basket near the un-lit fireplace.

Their instructor, a woman at least twenty years older than Shelley, with silver white hair in a bun and a peaceful air floated into the room. She smiled serenely. But her glance was filled with concern as she noted Ric's street clothes and holstered weapon. Once Bliss, Ava, and Jess were in the room, Ric nodded at Shelley and slipped outside to guard the entrance.

The yoga class went a long way toward easing Shelley's tension.

But as soon as they opened the doors, there was Ric. Standing guard. Standing at attention. The stress and the awkward that she'd managed to bend and twist her way out of during yoga came hurtling back.

After facials and massages, they were served lunch in the Aquavant room with the hydro-spa. Humidity simmered in the private pool room.

Ric tried to sit unobtrusively in the corner but Shelley was hyperaware of him. Her body instinctively knew where he was in each room she had been in. He exuded a sexuality that sparked her own visceral awareness of him.

It had been easier to ignore him when she'd had her eyes closed during her massage and facial. But as the women sat at the dining table in spa robes, Shelley couldn't ignore the way her body reacted to his commanding masculine presence.

A spa staff member served their pre-ordered lunches at the small table.

Shelley picked at her salad. The greens were fresh. The tomatoes and cucumber crisp. The chicken grilled and still warm. The vinaigrette lightly seasoned. But she was so unsettled that everything seemed off and she barely ate. At this rate, she'd lose that extra five pounds that always seemed to linger on her hips.

The girls drank a light white wine while Shelley stuck to water.

After lunch, they submersed in the deliciously scented pool, relaxing in the warm salt water, while Ric continued to stand guard.

Shelley lay back against the edge of the pool, her head rested on the lip and her body floated in the warm soothing water but she couldn't unwind. The tension of the day had manifested in her stomach and she pressed her hand to her belly wishing she could just relax.

Ric noted her movement. "You okay?"

"I'm fine." She couldn't even have a moment. He was that observant.

Of course, his observation skills had paid off tremendously last night. She flushed and hoped the steam from the pool would disguise the fact that she was getting slightly turned on.

From outside their private room, a woman was complaining loudly about the fact that her trip to the pool was delayed. That was thanks to them.

Oddly something about the woman's voice, or maybe her whine, registered with Shelley. "I don't see why some people get special treatment."

Shelley opened her eyes and lifted her head as the door rattled.

Ric was across the room and in front of the ornate doors in a heartbeat. He had his weapon out and ready. Her body tightened. She couldn't imagine that someone complaining about a hydro therapy bath was a threat. But what if she was? Ric was standing right in the way.

"You need to leave this room alone," the spa employee said to whoever was on the other side of the door.

"Fine, but don't think the manager won't hear about this." The voice faded as if the complainer was walking away from the room.

Everyone relaxed.

Ric didn't return to his seat. He stood next to the door, his body ready.

Shelley let her gaze trail lightly over him. His shoulders were broad and sturdy. His stomach flat, pecs rippled beneath the simple Polo shirt. His worn jeans cupped the bulge beneath his zipper and molded to thighs as thick as the eucalyptus trunks in her yard. His biceps tested the hem of his shirt sleeves, and dark hair dusted his forearms. A wide, black tactical watch emphasized his thick wrists, and drew her gaze to his hands. Those hands had caressed and stroked every single inch of her body, taking her to heights of pleasure that she'd never experienced before.

The memory of all that man between her thighs swept over her and her entire body liquefied in remembered lust.

Ric's gaze found hers, heated. But all he said was, "I'm going to step outside for a moment. I'll be right back." He nodded to all of the women.

"But we know it was a man that wrecked my hotel room." Shelley understood caution but that was definitely a woman's voice.

"It was too neat. He could have an accomplice. Or he could have been hired by a woman. At this point we can't rule out any possibilities."

Then he was gone.

"Someone's a little hot and bothered." Bliss's dark gaze shifted from Shelley to where Ric had just been standing. Shelley wanted to sink under the water in total embarrassment. Hopefully the flush on her face would be attributed to the moist heat of the pool rather than being turned on.

Jess laughed softly. "She should be. I saw him naked." She fanned her face with her fingers.

"Jess," Shelley hissed.

"I'd ask more questions, but we're talking about my mother-in-law-to-be." Bliss teased.

"Cut her a break," Ava said. "Con is freaked out by the whole thing."

Bliss frowned. "Yeah, Jack too." Her smile fell from her face and shadows darkened her eyes.

Shelley wondered at Bliss's expression. She thought that Bliss had been unnaturally subdued today but she really didn't know her future daughter-in-law that well. "Everything okay, honey?"

Bliss blinked furiously. "Of course. What could be wrong?"

"I don't know. Why don't you tell us?" Shelley said softly.

"I just…." Bliss pulled her legs in to her chest in, wrapped her arms around her calves, and rested her cheek on her knees.

They all waited, sensing that something important was coming. "Why isn't Jack taking care of your security?"

Shelley had wondered the same thing. Did it really make sense for Ric Santana to watch her? However, she didn't think that's what had really upset Bliss.

"And?"

"I think he's having second thoughts," Bliss whispered. Her words were barely audible over the rush of the bubbles in the pool.

"What?!" Jess sat up so quickly that water splashed over the edge and onto the tile floor.

"No way." Ava shook her head violently.

Shelley curled her arm around Bliss's shoulders. Her body was tight with tension. "Why do you think that?"

"Because he's been really distant and distracted since we got here." Bliss tucked her head down hiding her face from them all. "And I just can't help but feel like maybe he's changed his mind."

"He's *loco* over you." Ava patted Bliss's shoulder. She

pressed her lips together. "I work with him every day. I know what he's like when you're not around. He's not going to change his mind."

"Gotta agree with Ava on this one. Although you do make a good point about having Ric do mom's security," Jess said.

"You should just talk to him," Shelley counseled. "Ask him what's wrong."

"We were apart for a really long time." Bliss sighed. "It's possible that he's changed his mind. Maybe now that the initial blush of lost love is over, he's figured out he doesn't really want me."

Shelley hated the catch in Bliss's voice. She didn't for a moment think Jack was having second thoughts. But until Bliss brought it up, she hadn't really thought about the fact that Jack could have done her security. Of course, Shelley hadn't argued because she really didn't want to take over Jack's vacation time before the wedding. But maybe it was time to have a quick talk with her oldest son.

Her stomach rolled and another wave of heat flushed through her. But this time it wasn't from arousal.

Shelley jerked as her stomach did another slosh but this time it was more like a washing machine in spin cycle.

"You okay, mom?" Jess asked.

"I—" Her stomach protested. Suddenly, she knew if she didn't get out of this pool, she was in trouble. She shoved out of the water and sprinted for the small garbage can in the corner.

"Ric," Ava called out.

He burst back into the room just as Shelley lost the small amount of lunch she'd managed to force down.

"What the hell happened?" Ric barked out.

Shelley continued to puke in the small can. Bile burned

in her nose and humiliation swept through her. Wonderful. Was it possible to be any more embarrassed?

Ric placed his palm on her forehead.

Clammy sweat coated her skin and slicked his warm palm. "You okay, *cariña?*"

She nodded. But then a throbbing, pounding hit her head, and Shelley dry-heaved for another thirty seconds.

"That was weird. All the sudden I felt sick."

"I hope you aren't coming down with something." Bliss stroked her palm over Shelley's back.

"How sudden?" Ric asked suspiciously.

"One second I was fine and the next I…wasn't."

Ric stalked to the table. "Which dish is yours?"

"The salad." Ava pointed to Shelley's plate.

"You didn't eat much."

"I wasn't that hungry."

"You aren't doing some stupid thing where you don't eat before the wedding are you?" Ric asked harshly.

She wanted to take offense but she also wanted to laugh. "No."

"You didn't eat dinner last night and you barely ate any breakfast," Ric said.

Shelley flushed. But this time it was from embarrassment when all three of the girls snickered, clearly recalling why she didn't eat dinner.

"Do we really need to discuss my eating habits right now?" Shelley ducked her head.

"Why didn't you eat?" He wouldn't let it go.

She shrugged. "I felt a little off so I stopped."

Ric picked up the plate using the linen placemat to keep from touching the ceramic dish and handed it to Bliss. "I need you to have Jack get this analyzed."

Shelley's embarrassment fled. "What?"

"Maybe there's a reason you felt off." Ric curled his fingers into a fist. "I think it's time for you to go back to the room."

Bliss, Ava, and Jess were nodding, somber looks on their faces.

"You," she faltered then forced herself to continue. "You think my salad was drugged?"

"I'd like to get it tested." Ric didn't exactly answer her question. "In the meantime, you should probably go upstairs and lie down until we get a report on exactly what was on or in that salad."

Shelley's head spun. He really thought someone had drugged her food. Good gracious, what if someone else had eaten her salad? She needed to get away from the girls before something happened to one of them.

CHAPTER 10

$\mathcal{R}$ic paced the suite.

He was pissed because Shelley had been poisoned on his watch. All day, he'd been distracted by her. Finally in that private pool room, he kept getting preoccupied by Shelley in her demure, and frankly, what should have been unsexy, swimsuit. He'd missed something.

Fuck. He shouldn't have let Shelley go to the spa at all.

Ric stared at the toxicology report from her lunch. Jack had been able to get the results rushed. Shelley had been poisoned. There had been traces of Tetrahydrozoline in her salad. Someone had dripped Visine, fucking over-the-counter Visine, on the lettuce. Fortunately she hadn't eaten much so she'd only had a mild reaction to the chemical. If she'd eaten more, she'd have been in the hospital, but it most likely wouldn't have killed her. Which just made the whole situation a little more weird.

"I'm sorry, amigo."

Jack was slumped on the sofa, looking as worn out as Ric felt. "What the hell are you sorry for?"

After resting for the last few hours, Shelley was taking a shower, so Ric could speak freely. "I should have anticipated something like this. The entire day felt off." He'd attributed his uneasiness to the awkwardness of the situation. Initially he'd been caught up in protecting Shelley but as the day wore on and the threat level seemed to recede, other less professional thoughts had crowded his mind.

Shelley was absolutely stunning in her conservative swim suit that was more appropriate for doing laps than lounging by the pool. He'd known he needed to get out of that room when he'd started day dreaming about him and Shelley in the pool naked and doing decidedly un-spa-like activities.

His body had heated and his cock had hardened. He needed to act like the professional he was so, at the time, stepping out seemed like a good call.

Feeling slightly trapped, Ric had used the woman complaining to exit the private room for a moment. A note in that woman's voice had set him on edge. He wanted to see if he could catch a glimpse of her. His gaze had tracked along the ceiling to see if they had cameras in the spa's hallway. They didn't, but hopefully there was film of her at the spa entrance or in the reception area.

He hadn't liked the spa's set up. Too many unknown people who couldn't be vetted even though they were in different rooms than Shelley. Turned out he'd been right to worry since she'd fallen ill.

Now, he flipped through the photos of all the spa guests for the day. "Any of these women, or men, look familiar?"

Jack shook his head. "No. We'll have Shelley take a look when she's done."

He didn't like the suspicions that were swirling around in his mind. Something about the whole situation seemed…off.

Ransacking her hotel room. Poisoning her with a non-lethal dose of Tetrahydrozoline.

"It never occurred to me that the attacks would escalate this fast," Jack said.

"What the fuck is going on?" Ric slapped the report against his palm. Frustration and temper crested in a wave.

"Well this definitely adds suspicion of an accomplice," Jack commented.

Ric stared out the window at the skyline. "Yeah. While there were some men at the spa, the clientele were mostly women. Historically women were more likely to use poison than men although I'm not sure that holds true now. Plus it was only enough to incapacitate her. And we have no proof that the woman outside the private pool room was anything more than a disgruntled customer."

Jack paced around the room. "I wish I had some idea of what the hell is going on."

The door to the bathroom opened.

Shelley exited in a cloud of steam. Ric admired the completely unselfconscious sway of her hips. She was wearing the hotel's thick cotton robe and he nearly swallowed his tongue.

She struck him mute when she headed straight to his side. "Are you okay?"

In his line of work, he needed a serious poker face. He never showed emotion. It was one of the issues that had come up regularly back when he'd been trying to have relationships. His girlfriends never had any idea what he was thinking. They'd complained more often than not that he didn't share his feelings.

Shelley had picked up on his hidden distress after knowing him less than a day. That was shocking.

"I'm fine. Nothing is wrong." Ric threaded his fingers

with hers and squeezed. "I'm not going to let anything happen to you," he said fiercely.

"Oh. I know you won't." Shelley disengaged their fingers.

As if his capability was never in question. She'd wiped out his frustration with four simple words. She believed he would keep her safe. Ric vowed right then and there that he wouldn't let her down.

Her entire body stiffened, then she frowned. "Hi, Jack."

"Shel." Jack nodded sternly.

"We've got the pictures of the women and men who were in the spa while you were there." Ric gestured at the sofa. "Have a seat and we'll go through them."

The spa didn't have cameras in their interior hallways, only in the waiting room slash reception area. He'd printed pictures of all the people who had gone in and out while Shelley and the girls were getting their treatments. But unless Shelley could identify any of the people, right now it was a dead end.

Twenty minutes later, Shelley hadn't been able to identify any single person. So the pictures were a bust. At least for now.

But she fidgeted on the sofa. Something else was going on. Ric watched Shelley closely.

"Um, Jack, I need to talk to you." She wasn't twisting her hands but her demeanor was one step up from a worried mother.

"Shoot."

Shelley darted a furtive glance at Ric. "Alone." She blinked, her lashes covering her gaze and creating a shadow over her cheeks.

Ric puffed up his chest ready to argue but Jack beat him to it.

"Listen, Shel. Ric needs to hear whatever you have to say."

Her face flushed red. Whatever she needed to say, she was seriously embarrassed. Ric supposed he should have offered to leave the room, but after this morning, he had no intention of leaving her alone again.

"He can't protect you if you keep things from—"

"Bliss thinks you're having second thoughts," she blurted out. She jumped up from the sofa and propped her hands on her hips.

Jack bunched his fists. "What?"

"Normally I wouldn't get involved in your relationship." Shelley said, "But she was really upset earlier."

"She...."

"Thinks you're reconsidering the wedding." Shelley said softly, "You need to talk to her, Jack."

"Why would she think that?" The true bewilderment and sense of panic on Jack's face was a revelation. Ric had never seen his buddy so gone over a woman. He supposed that's why Jack was getting married.

"Well," Shelley shot an inscrutable look at Ric before shifting her attention back to her stepson.

"Come on, Shel."

"She wondered why you aren't doing my security." If he wasn't mistaken, Shelley was feeling guilty for questioning why Ric was doing her security. Not that he minded.

She mouthed, Sorry.

Ric froze. He knew why Jack wasn't watching out for his stepmother. He was on a very private, very personal mission.

Ric exchanged a significant glance with Jack.

Shelley shifted her gaze back and forth between the two of them. "What?"

"What, what?" Jack said.

"What was that look?" Shelley directed her question to Ric already figuring out that Jack wasn't going to say a word. But it wasn't Ric's secret to share. Before Ric could reply, Jack butt in. "How could she think that?"

Shelley shrugged. "You haven't been back together that long."

Jack shook his head.

"When you know, you *know*. It hits you right here." Jack thumped his fist over his heart. "I need to go."

Shelley nodded. "Talk to her."

Ric eyed Jack. "The Visine is a dead end." There was no way they could track every single purchase in the area and that assumed it was bought in Las Vegas. "But Con is continuing to trace emails."

"We good?" Jack asked.

"I've got it."

Shelley rubbed her palms over her biceps. "What about the dinner tonight?"

"What dinner tonight?" Rick asked.

"Family dinner," Jack said tersely. "I didn't invite you because I thought you'd want some of your own time in Vegas."

Ah. That made sense. But if Shelley was going to a family dinner, there's no way he'd let her go without him.

"I'd like to go," Shelley said.

"How are you feeling?" Ric asked.

"My stomach is still a little queasy. But better than I was."

"The only way I'd be comfortable with you attending is if I'm also there." Ric refused to budge on that point.

"Private room. Don't have to leave the hotel." Jack gave the details. "I'm placing people, actually two, in the kitchen."

Ric nodded. "Okay. Then you can go."

Shelley bristled beside him. But there was no way in hell he was letting her out of his sight. "We'll hang here until the dinner."

"But—"

"No arguing." Ric was adamant. "Your safety is the most important issue."

Besides, she needed to rest.

"I'm out," Jack said.

After Jack left there was an uncomfortable silence in the room. He'd just insisted that he and Shelley spend the next few hours here and not leave.

She plopped down on the sectional sofa that overlooked the Vegas skyline. "Can you tell me why Jack is having you do my security?"

He tried not to let her lack of confidence in his skills bother him. "It's not my secret to share."

Shelley sighed and her shoulders slumped. The neckline of her robe gaped open just enough to show the alabaster curve of her breast. Ric swallowed and turned his focus to the scenery rather than Shelley's hot body. The smoking attraction that arced between them all day shot from low simmer to white hot electric.

"However I can absolutely guarantee that it is the exact opposite of him having second thoughts." His pal was one hundred and fifty percent hung up on his fiancee.

So much so that Ric envied his pal's commitment.

"Good." She smiled softly. "That's good. Jack deserves to be happy."

There she went again with other people deserving things. But that wasn't a conversation they needed to have right now. Shelley rubbed her palm over her abdomen.

"You doing okay?"

"Besides the fact that someone tried to poison me?" Shelley quipped.

Ric's stomach turned at the reality that someone had succeeded. They hadn't wanted her dead. Otherwise....

Damn, the thought that she could be hurt, burned like acid on his skin.

Ric needed to touch her. To reassure himself that for now she was okay. He sat on the sofa and curled his arm around her shoulders somewhat tentatively, but then she turned and practically threw herself into his embrace. Her head butted his collarbone and she wrapped her arms tightly around his waist.

"How did you order your lunch?" Ric turned over details in his brain, searching for the right fact. The one that would cause all the other elements to fall in place and create an actionable picture. For now all they had were random acts and random threats, but nothing that tied it all together.

"We pre-ordered ahead of time," Shelley replied.

"So they targeted you." But again they didn't give her enough to kill her. Just enough to get her out of the way. "Before you got to Vegas did you have any other overt threats?"

Shelley snorted. "Nope."

A shiver worked its way over her body and she curled into his heat. "What about tonight? No one else got sick today but what if they try again tonight and hurt one of the kids?"

Ric hated to see her so upset. He rested his chin on her head.

"I couldn't stand it if someone got hurt because of me."

"Hey." Ric inhaled the sweet floral scent of her shampoo, the fragrance invading his senses. "We're on top of it. Besides there wasn't enough to actually kill you. It was just supposed to incapacitate you."

Which again was sort of weird. Almost as if they just wanted to scare her away. Ric rubbed his palm over her back and tried not to notice her warm naked skin pressed against his chest.

"Did you have any attempts while you were still in Monterey?"

Shelley shook her head, her damp hair rubbed his chin. "No."

So perhaps they were just trying to scare her away from Las Vegas. "Why would someone want you away from Vegas?"

Ric shifted so that his legs stretched out on the sectional sofa and Shelley twined her bare legs with his. The hem of the white cotton robe rode up until the back of her knees were exposed. Hardly an erotic sight, but Ric was remembering last night. Shelley laid out on the rumpled sheets, those gorgeous toned thighs bracketing his face as he devoured her pussy.

The sounds she'd made as she was coming were indelibly imprinted on his brain.

Just thinking about those damn noises had his cock rising. He couldn't have sex with his principal. It wasn't a safe move. But damn he wanted to bury his face in her sex and lick and suck until she was writhing beneath him, begging him to make her come.

Shelley shifted then went motionless as she felt his erection.

Ric held back a groan when instead of shifting away she stroked her belly against his straining hardness.

They were both panting. Shelley had burrowed her

hands beneath his cotton Polo and smoothed her palms over his abs and chest. She was burning him up.

He rolled her so that she was sandwiched between the back of the sofa and his body. With a deep groan, he buried his face in the curve of her neck and breathed her in. He couldn't take this any further, but he needed a moment to get a grip.

Shelley twined her legs with his and stroked his cock through his jeans.

"We can't." He protested.

A loud knock at the door startled them both.

Shelley jumped off the sofa so fast she swayed, perilously close to falling over.

"Lock yourself in the bathroom. If you hear anything suspicious, climb in the tub and use the phone to call security." He shot instructions at her like bullets. Ric eased his weapon from the holster and headed to the door, covering his bases, even though he doubted her perpetrator would just knock on the door.

The banging got louder. "Shelley!"

Connor. Cockblocked by her stepson. Ric still peered through the peephole to verify it was indeed Connor Stone. The guy had impeccable timing.

Connor's grim face stared back at him. Ric unlocked the door and let him in.

"What took so long?" Connor growled.

"Con?" Shelley came out of the bathroom, still in the short robe, her hair mussed and her lips reddened. "Is everything okay?"

Connor's attention shifted between Shelley's attire and Ric. He scowled at Ric who fought the urge to smooth his hand over his hair. Shelley was a grown woman, dammit.

"You took forever to answer the door," Connor finally replied.

Shelley flushed. "Ric was just being extra cautious."

"I'll bet he was."

"Was there a reason you stopped by?" Ric tried to divert Shelley's focus away from Connor's sarcasm.

Connor blinked. "Oh, uh, yeah. I found four email addresses that I want you to take a look at."

They sat on the sectional sofa. Shelley intuitively returned to the spot she'd just vacated. Ric had a primitive compulsion to be close to her. He forced himself to sit at an angle so that Connor could show her the addresses. "By analyzing several variables, language, tone, and type of message, I was able to distill all the possible matches down to these four as potential matches."

He had printouts of each address along with the emails sent. Ric leaned closer so he could read the contents. "Can you look at these and see if you know the senders?"

Shelley studied the four sheets.

"Are any based in Las Vegas?" Ric asked.

Shelley was so close that he could see the small mole at the corner of her mouth. She must cover it up with makeup most of the time because he hadn't noticed it before.

Her scent rose from her skin and he lost himself in the bottomless pools of her eyes.

Connor cleared his throat, and they broke apart. "Why Vegas?"

"I've been thinking about it." Ric concluded, "Prior to coming to Vegas all the love letters and threats had been verbal or written. No physical contact. But since Shelley arrived here, there's been an escalation."

Both acts against her seemed perpetrated with the aim

of getting her to leave Las Vegas. "Why would someone want you gone from here?"

"I don't know."

Connor said, "You recognize any of the screen names associated with these email addresses, maybe from another form of social media or as a nickname for someone you know?"

"No." Her heart was beating so hard that her breastbone shook her entire chest.

"Hey, it's just a line of investigation." Ric covered her hand, squeezed her fingers, amazed all over again at how delicate she was once you got past the force of her personality.

"Good point." Con nodded. "Two of the addresses are from Vegas but both have decent security."

Shelley shivered.

"Shel, you know we would never let anything happen to you." Connor consoled her.

"Oh, sweetie." Shelley's smile was bittersweet. "I'm more worried about all you kids."

"We're hardly children." Connor hesitated for a second, then patted her hand. "Don't worry, I will figure this out."

"Everyone is working to make sure you're safe." Ric couldn't help but add. But if anything that seemed to make Shelley more uncomfortable. And he understood. She didn't like being the center of attention. He got that. He preferred to travel under the radar too.

"It's almost as if we're dealing with two different perpetrators." Connor frowned.

Ric rubbed his hand over the back of his neck. So far his relaxing vacation was turning out to be higher stress than he'd anticipated. "I'll keep her physically safe. Think you can handle the cyber aspect?"

"I'm going to run a different analysis program and see if I can get a legal name and location for all four of these addresses."

"Sounds good." Ric shook Connor's hand.

It may have been his imagination but it seemed as if Connor squeezed a little too long during the shake. Another warning. What Connor hadn't seemed to figure out was that Ric would do anything to keep Shelley safe.

CHAPTER 11

She didn't have a good feeling about this.

Shelley and Ric entered the private dining room at the steakhouse. They walked in to the dimly lit, atmospheric restaurant.

Ric had placed a possessive hand at the small of her back, his fingertips burned through the thin material of the sexy black dress. Desire sizzled in a direct line from his fingertips to her clit. She'd spent extra time on her makeup and slathered a shimmery lotion over her bare arms and legs hoping to distract herself from the real worry that she was putting everyone in danger.

Shelley recalled the last time she was here. She was wearing the same LBD and heels that she'd worn just last night.

It seemed almost impossible that she'd only been here twenty-four hours ago with Ric. The sexy stranger. Now he was Ric, her sexy bodyguard, and they had barely been out of each other's sight. With that thought her muscles twisted into a bunched mass of frustration and fear.

She'd coiled her hair up into a complicated twist leaving her neck bare.

"It's going to be fine," Ric murmured in her ear. His breath puffed over her neck and goose bumps skittered across her arms. The hum of spirited conversations greeted their arrival as Ric had Shelley precede him into the private dining room.

"Shel." Jack pushed back from the head of the table. Her protector was all grown up and in charge. She really hoped Jack and Bliss had worked out whatever was wrong. Bliss rose from the table, stunning in a little black silk dress with a Mandarin collar and red silk accents, silk buttons down the front, and black patent Louboutins with the signature red sole. Shelley noted that the strain around her dark exotic eyes, high cheekbones, and tight smile hadn't gone away.

Shelley impulsively hugged Bliss. "It will be okay."

"I think that's supposed to be my line," Bliss said ruefully.

Jack slapped Ric on the back in a man hug, and they spoke quietly. So quietly, Shelley couldn't hear a word.

"Looking good, mom." Jess hugged her tightly. "How are you doing?"

"Better."

Colin kissed her left cheek, then her right. "Always here if you need another bodyguard, love."

Shelley squeezed him in an appreciative hug. "Thank you."

Jess held Colin's hand loosely in hers. Shelley was thankful her daughter seemed happy, settled. Although she worried a little about Jess working for Jack, she also knew that Jess could take care of herself.

Shelley glanced around the room. "Where's John?"

"He's working an angle on finding Fernandez's contact in Vegas," Jack explained. "For right now, we aren't advertising that he is part of the family. He's staying in a condo with Maria and Marissa who works with Bliss at Adams Larsen."

Bottles of corked wine sat at even intervals on the table. Platters of seafood, calamari, oysters, and tuna were scattered at each end.

"Did someone vet the food?" Ric was in full protection mode. Though they were in a private room with just family, he hadn't moved far from her side.

"Shane and Keisha volunteered to observe in the kitchen."

"So, no break in the chain of custody."

Shelley snorted. "Did you really just call serving appetizers—"

"I take your safety very seriously," he whispered in her ear. The tingle skittered over her spine. "And I won't let anyone hurt you. Or your family."

The conviction in his voice was like a balm to her rattled nerves.

Before she could say thank you, Connor and Ava walked into the room. Together they were striking. Ava with her thick black hair and darker skin and Con with his blond hair and unusual golden brown eyes. Shelley's heart melted at the soft look on Con's face as he gazed at Ava.

Greetings were exchanged. The atmosphere in the room was downright festive. They sat at the large rectangular table and started passing the appetizers. Ric was on her right at one end of the table, his body like an inferno, and his thigh seemed awfully close to hers. His presence was distracting. Connor was on her left with Ava next to him. Jack sat at the head of the table with Bliss on his left. Jess and Colin sat across from Con and Shelley.

Shelley observed Jack. He appeared to still be carrying a lot of stress. She hoped that whatever was going on between him and Bliss worked itself out. Jack deserved to be happy.

Con reached over and clasped her hand in a quick squeeze. "How are you?"

His gaze slipped to the proximity of Ric's body to hers. Shelley tried unobtrusively to ease away, but Ric tugged on her chair until she was closer to him. "Sorry to be causing so much trouble," she started.

Before Shelley could say anything else, a bleach blonde woman dressed in black skinny jeans, stiletto heels and a blue sequined tube top, burst into the room.

"Connor, baby. Is that you?" She squealed in a baby doll voice that was more suited to a teenager and threw her arms wide open. Shelley wasn't sure how old the woman was, her face had been slightly distorted by plastic surgery so she could be anywhere from thirty to sixty.

Her body had likely been altered too. She was thin with large breasts. Something about her was familiar, but Shelley couldn't figure out why she thought that.

Beside Connor, Ava froze. Connor discreetly laced his fingers with Ava's.

Connor cleared his throat. "Do I know you?"

Shelley studied the shape of the woman's chin and her eyes as they filled with false tears. Finally she figured out how she knew the woman. She'd only met her once, a long time ago, but she was pretty sure it was Kandi.

"Do you *know* me?" She scooted around the table and flung herself at Connor. "I'm your mama."

Everyone in the room stuttered to a halt. Con had gone stock still. Not moving. Not breathing. Bliss and Colin's mouths were both hanging open. Jack looked ready to murder her. Ava was trying unsuccessfully to tug her fingers from Connor's but he was holding on too tightly. Ric just sat silently, observing.

So it looked like was up to Shelley to salvage the situation.

She stood smoothly trying desperately to control the urge to bitch slap the woman. Con so did not need this right now. "Kandi, I don't think this is the proper time—"

"I was talking to my son." Kandi tilted her head down as if she were looking over a pair of glasses frames, her unnaturally blue eyes stared at Connor with an unholy light.

Shelley tried, patiently to shove down her rage. This woman was not going to ruin Con's vacation. And calling him her son was a bit of a stretch, since she'd only been back once in the last twenty years and that was to ask for more money. She'd timed that visit for when the kids were at school so Con hadn't seen his mother while she'd been trying to extort more cash from an absent Jackson Sr.

However, Shelley wasn't going to stop Con from visiting with his mother if he wished. But she knew her adopted son well enough to know he would hate being the center of this kind of attention.

Always trying to be the peacemaker, Shelley tried to fix this. She pasted on her accommodating, lady of the manor, 'you won't hurt me with your superior attitude and misplaced jealousy' smile that she'd perfected all those years ago when she'd first moved into the Stone mansion and used it to try to put Kandi at ease. "Why not make arrangements to meet sometime later?"

Con shoved his chair away from the table and stood. "What are you doing here?"

Kandi threaded her arm through Con's and leaned into

her biological son. Her cobalt blue sequined top showcased her purchased cleavage prominently, as she stared at Con and blinked her false black lashes. "Baby, I live in Vegas."

Jack started toward Kandi, which was not going to end well. But before he could take more than one step, Con held his palm up to stop his brother. "I've got this."

Her acrylic nails were the same unnatural blue as her eyes and obscenely gaudy next to Con's understated navy blazer. He carefully peeled her fingers from his forearm. "I meant, Kandi," his voice was a low growl, "what are you doing in this room?"

"I saw the family name on the waitress podium out front." Kandi was definitely not comprehending the angry vibe rolling off Connor. He was pissed.

When Shelley looked at him, she didn't see a grown man, rather the bewildered child he'd been when Shelley had shown up on Jackson Stone's doorstep all those years ago. Because she knew how sensitive he was and how much it would pain him if he yelled at his mother, Shelley intervened. Her only thought was to protect Connor.

"I think it would be best if you exchanged numbers," Shelley started.

Kandi ignored her. Didn't even look at Shelley.

"Shel, stop." Con gently brushed his palm over her shoulder then turned to Kandi. "What do you want?"

"I couldn't believe it when I saw your name," Kandi simpered. "I had to see you."

Shelley opened her mouth but nothing came out. She quivered with the urge to get in Kandi's face and give her a piece of her mind. How dare she mess with Connor like this?

She jolted when Ric tugged her back into her chair and draped his arm casually over her shoulders. She was probably the only one who knew there was nothing simple or casual about his hold. She wouldn't be able to break free.

"I'll make this as clear as possible," Connor said softly. "Leave."

Finally Kandi got that Connor wasn't happy. "We can exchange numbers."

"I don't think you understand." Connor folded his arms over his chest, his shoulders bulked. "Don't call. Don't come back. Ever."

"But," Kandi sputtered. "Connor, baby. You can't mean that. I'm your mama."

"You are nothing but an egg donor," Connor replied calmly.

"But—"

"Shelley," he placed his palm on Shelley's shoulder and squeezed, "is my mother. The only mother I want or need."

Shelley's heart swelled. She tilted her head so her cheek brushed his hand.

"You can't possibly mean that." Kandi stomped her stiletto booted foot, her enhanced breasts jiggled and her face twisted into an ugly mask.

"I absolutely mean it. She's an angel." Connor smiled.

But Kandi wasn't done. "*I'm* your mother."

Shelley thought Kandi might actually launch herself at Connor.

Ric jumped in front of Kandi and subdued her with one quick action. Shelley hadn't seen him move. He held Kandi's arm in an iron grip. "You need to leave."

"But—"

Ric said calmly, "Call security."

Kandi tried to wrench her arm away but his hold didn't budge. "Forget it. I'll leave."

Ric and Jack exchanged a pointed look. "You okay with that, Connor?"

Con sighed wearily. "Just let her go."

Ric escorted her to the door. Just as he was about to get her out of the room, their waitress rolled in a cart with the first course and stopped just inside the doorway. She looked confused at the group of people clustered around the entrance. In that moment of distraction, Kandi tugged her arm from Ric's hold and almost ran in to Shane Washington.

Behind Shane, hovering on the other side of the doorway, stood a bulky man in an Armani suit, hair military short, and craggy blunt features. The man hadn't been visible until the waitress opened the door.

Once the waitress and Shane were between Kandi and the rest of the room, Kandi shot Shelley a venomous glare. Shelley recoiled at the visible hatred in Kandi's gaze.

"Let's go, Kandi," her male friend spoke. He grabbed her hand and tugged her toward the exit.

That had certainly been weird. Her trip to Las Vegas was just one bizarre happening after another. She hated to imagine what could happen next.

But in typical fashion, Shelley tried to put everyone back at ease.

Her stomach was a mess, between the remnants of her drugged salad, and the sickly acid from this last confrontation, she'd be happy not eating for a week.

"Who's hungry?"

Ric stared after Kandi and her companion and then made a dash for the entrance. Jack shot out of his chair too. But the cart and Shane blocked their exit, and by the time they got around the obstacle and ran through the restaurant, it was too late.

CHAPTER 12

*W*hat a clusterfuck.

As soon as Ric saw Kandi's companion, he put it all together. They might be Shelley's stalkers. After all, what were the odds that Con's mother would show up at the same time that Shelley started having all her problems?

He and Jack had come to the realization at the same time and taken off after the pair but it had been too late. After searching the casino floor, they finally returned to the restaurant, frustrated and subdued. He and Jack had both made calls and notified security, but no one had been able to find either Kandi or the guy. Ric had called his computer guy to run a check on Kandi but he didn't have her companion's name. So far, his guy hadn't turned up much beyond a crap ton of credit card bills and an apartment in Vegas.

Connor had been quiet through the rest of dinner. Of Jack's siblings, Connor was the brother Ric knew least. Army vs. Navy. But Jack had never spoken of his brother with anything but admiration and maybe a little exasperation.

If only Ric had put it together sooner. But Kandi hadn't acknowledged Shelley at any time during her interaction with Connor until that very last vitriolic look.

Which led Ric right back to his current problem. This wasn't going to be a fun convo.

While Shelley was in the bathroom, he quietly dialed Jack. "Tell me you got a picture of Kandi's friend."

"Yep," Jack said. "I'm running it through the facial comparison program now."

"There was something about the way he moved." Ric mused. "Did you see it?"

"I thought so too," Jack said. "Good call. It is him."

So Kandi's friend was the one who trashed Shelley's hotel room.

Although Shelley's protection duty had only started this morning, he was ready to have this particular job over with. Sitting next to Shelley tonight at dinner had been torture. Every time she moved in that dress, he remembered the night before.

She was unbelievably sensual.

He wanted to eat her up. But first they had to catch the people harassing her.

"So it's likely Kandi was working with him to try to scare Shelley away."

"What the hell is her end game?" Jack snarled.

"Hopefully the cops can round them up quickly and we can find out." Ric let relief swell over him. This would be over with soon. Ric hesitated which pissed him off. He wasn't the hesitating type. "What about Connor?"

Jack barked out a laugh. "What?"

"It has to be asked." Ric paced to the bed and back as he ran his fingers through his hair.

That shut Jack up. "You can't really think—"

"Doing the job you asked me to do, Jack."

"Shit. You're right. Even though you're wrong. There's absolutely no way my brother had anything to do with whatever is going on with his biological egg donor." Jack blew out a frustrated breath. "Fuck."

"I need to have a chat with him." Logically Ric didn't believe that Connor Stone had anything to do with the threats to Shelley. But he wouldn't be doing the job Jack asked him to do, the job he'd vowed to do, if he didn't pursue the lead.

"I'll call him," Jack said. "I need to prep him."

Ric didn't like the idea of giving Connor a heads up but he understood Jack's reasoning.

"I'll send him down." Jack said, "You keep watch on Shelley while I work with the police."

"I'm not going anywhere," Ric said fiercely.

"Thanks, BP."

Ric heard the strain in Jack's voice. He had been aware of the distance between Bliss Lee and Jack tonight at dinner. "You make any headway on that other project?"

"I thought I did but it was a dead end and I'm running out of time," Jack said wearily.

"You may want to come clean with your fiancée."

Of course, what did he know about fiancées? His failed marriage had been over years ago.

"Giving it a few more days." Jack was unable to let go of his hope. "Later, BP."

Ric hung up and waited for Con to arrive.

Shelley emerged from the bathroom. She had changed from her dress into a pair of running shorts and a t-shirt. There was nothing overtly sexy about the outfit and still every nerve in his body came to attention. Like a pointer dog on the trail of prey, his cock rose toward her.

Sweet mercy, it was going to be a long night.

A knock on the door interrupted his thoughts and Ric's cock deflated faster than a popped balloon. This was going to be ugly.

Shelley's head lifted from the magazine she was pretending to read on the sofa. "Who do you think it is?" Her eyes were wide and startled.

"Connor."

She shifted getting ready to answer the door but Ric held out his palm. "I'll get it."

He let Jack's younger half-brother into the room. Connor nodded tensely at Ric. He knew exactly why he was here.

Connor Stone was a wickedly smart man.

"Hi Con." Her smiled faded at the serious expression darkening the younger man's eyes.

Connor knelt next Shelley. "I'm sorry."

Right away Ric's hackles rose. What the fuck? Could Jack have been wrong?

"You have *nothing* to be sorry for." Shelley grabbed Con's hands and Ric immediately went for his weapon. "Put that away," she demanded.

Shelley ran her hand through Connor's hair.

"Shelley." Connor bowed his head. "I don't know what to say."

"Con, you are not responsible for her actions."

He hugged her tightly for a moment. Then, because he understood that Shelley's blind faith wasn't enough, he stood and addressed Ric, "What do you need?"

Ric nodded. "Just a few questions."

Shelley jumped up. Her heart was pounding so hard he could see her chest shake. "What are you talking about?"

Ric was pretty sure this conversation was going to deep

six any chance of sex in the future but if it kept Shelley safe then he'd forgo the extra hot hook up in a heartbeat. "I need to verify that Connor didn't have anything to do with your attacks."

Connor's mouth tightened but he nodded. Shelley on the other hand jumped in front of her adopted son as if to shield him from Ric's evil interrogation.

"Shelley." Ric's heart sunk.

"He had nothing to do with what happened."

Connor curled his palm around Shelley's wrist. "He's right to ask."

"No, he isn't," she said fiercely, a mama bear protecting her cub. She glared at Ric. Fantastic. He *definitely* wasn't getting laid any time soon.

"Have you had any contact with Kandi Kane recently?" And didn't that sound like something straight out of a porn flick? She must have legally changed her name.

Shelley fumed beside Connor.

He shook his head. "She came by the house once when I was around four. I vaguely remember it being...unpleasant."

Ric had a difficult relationship with his mother but at least she'd been around. And she loved him. He knew that even if they weren't particularly close.

"Any other contact?"

Con replied, "No."

"Would you be willing to submit your phone?" Ric asked.

"Sure." Connor reached into his pocket and pulled out his cell. "Here."

"Thanks." Although his surrender of his phone really proved nothing since Connor was a computer genius.

"You know that I could program my phone not to show specific contact information? Or I could have a burner."

All that was true. Connor was savvy enough to do it.

"This is absurd." Shelley curled her arm around Connor's shoulders. "He has nothing to do with Kandi and her issues."

Ric rubbed his palm over his face. "Shelley. Jack asked me to keep you safe. If I don't follow all potential trails, then I'm not doing my job."

Her mouth flattened into a tight line.

"So that was the first time you'd seen your mother in years?"

"Uh yeah." Connor looked ill at ease. "In the spirit of full disclosure, I did…look her up when I was about seventeen or eighteen. But I didn't have any contact with her."

"Oh, Con," Shelley said softly. "You could have asked me."

"Yeah, I wanted to do it on my own. But once I did some research I knew I didn't need to see her in person again."

"Sweetie." Shelley's green eyes filled with tears. "I'm so sorry."

"Not your fault she's a fucking gold digger." Con clenched his fists and his face contorted into a brutal frown. "I promise you. I will not let her hurt you."

"I know that." Shelley turned and glared at Ric. "This is done."

It was. Ric could see by the sheer affection between them and the way that Connor shielded Shelley from Ric that Connor would never hurt Shelley. "Can you, uh, stay in the room with Shelley, while I make a quick call?"

"Yeah." Con smiled.

Ric let himself out of the room.

Shelley paced around the sofa trying to burn off the frantic, angry energy that Ric's questioning had caused.

Neither one of them said anything for a few moments. Then she couldn't stand it anymore. "You know I had nothing to do with that, that travesty that just occurred."

"Shel, I'd be more worried if he didn't question me."

"Well that sucked. Of course you don't have anything to do with whatever is going on."

She kicked at something on the floor and it skipped across the carpet next to Connor's shoe. He picked up the crumpled condom package. Oh my God. The maid hadn't been allowed back in the room since the incident and somehow they'd missed one.

"Yours?" Connor raised one eyebrow.

"Oh my God." Her face burned. She'd blushed more in the past day than in the past twenty years. But there certainly wasn't going to be any more sex happening here now.

"At least you practiced safe sex." Con snickered.

"You want to think back a few months to me walking in on you and Ava?"

That shut him up.

"I thought not." She was mostly teasing him.

Con wrapped his arms around her shoulders and tugged her into a hug. No hesitation, no tentative pause before he showed her affection.

Shelley's heart melted at the fact that Con finally, finally embraced her with no hesitation. All it took was having her hotel room trashed, being poisoned, and threatened by her baby daddy's ex-girlfriend.

Shelley almost laughed.

"I'm glad you've got someone, Shel."

"It's only temporary." That truth hurt. It was realistic. It *was* only temporary. Their few hours of pleasure had somehow turned from a one night stand into a bizarre unexpected need for protection. Ric had promised to protect her body, but she wondered how she was going to protect her heart.

"You never know," he said softly. "It was killing him to have to interrogate me about Kandi. Because he knew it hurt you."

Shelley shrugged.

"Shel, he did it anyway, to keep you safe." Connor said, "It takes an honorable man to do what's right even if it will make things difficult for him."

"Aw, sweetie." Shelley hugged Connor. "I love you. You know that right?"

"I know." He rested his cheek against her hair. "Love you too."

In the oddest way, Kandi had managed to give Shelley something she'd been waiting and hoping would happen for years. Connor had finally fully accepted her.

CHAPTER 13

He was sick of these four walls.

Shelley paced around the suite, which yesterday had seemed fairly large. But after being confined for the past twenty-four hours while the police, and the extended Stone family, searched for Kandi had taken its toll.

In an odd twist, the boyfriend had come forward last night and turned himself in for trashing Shelley's hotel room. He'd had a massive fight with Kandi after they left the restaurant last night, and he'd gotten a look at the Stone family.

He knew when to cut his losses. So he'd confessed to the crime, and today his attorney plead the charge down to the more minor misdemeanor charge plus a fine with no incarceration.

He also told the cops that Kandi was totally cray-cray. What he didn't know, was where Kandi had disappeared to.

He'd confessed about the same time that Con had broken the encryption on the Las Vegas emails. The poor guy was pretty broken up about the fact that his mother was the one who'd been harassing Shelley.

But now Kandi was in the wind.

Between him and Shelley hiding out in this damn room together, they were both beyond tense. The urge to jump her was growing stronger. He really wanted to lay her out on the bed and ravish her.

Never in his fucking life had he used the word ravish. He was going crazy and he was pretty sure Shelley wasn't far behind.

Not to mention the fact that she was still pissed at him for questioning Connor.

Shelley counted off the steps to the floor to ceiling windows. Then she paced to the sectional sofa. "You know I hate to complain, but I'm going nuts."

Before he could answer, she started babbling.

"Actually you don't know I hate to complain. Because you don't know me. But I do. I hate it. I'm used to being swamped."

Ric thought about security. He thought about Jack's influence. Maybe he could do something about their combined antsiness. They needed to get the hell out of this hotel room.

"Give me half an hour."

She stopped dead in the middle of the room. Interest, speculation lit up her bright green eyes. "For what?"

"I don't want to get your hopes up." Ric pressed a number on his cell.

It took more like forty-five minutes, but Ric managed to get them entrance into the closed fitness center and spa.

The security guard who escorted them to the secured facility and let them in admonished Ric, "Call when you're done. Use the phone at the desk. Your cell won't work in here. And please, don't leave a mess." Ric had a feeling this wasn't the first time he'd escorted guests into the supposedly closed spa.

The previously soothing reception area was bathed in darkness except for one soft spotlight over the registration desk. The fountain in the corner was silent.

"Oh my God." Shelley giggled, practically giddy with the forbidden. In her pale gray and neon yellow running shorts and tight gray and white spandex halter top, her sleek form taunted him. "I can't wait to get some action."

Action. He wanted to groan. He needed some serious physical action to keep his mind out of the gutter and off of getting some action with Shelley.

She bounced on her toes as she waited for him to open the doors to the exercise room. Ric quickly averted his gaze from the jiggle of her breasts. He tried to block the memory of her riding him, tits bobbing as she slammed down on him.

Ric wiped the sweat from his forehead with his forearm. Shit. Was it hot in here?

Shelley zoomed over to the treadmill and hopped on. Her ass, cupped lovingly by the shorts, swayed enticingly as she started a brisk warm up on the treadmill.

Ric figured that in the closed spa, with only the security staff and Jack knowing they were here, she was safe enough. However he was still armed. He placed his weapon on top of the water cooler next to an open treadmill. Ric vowed to stay alert. To keep his focus on the surroundings and off his principal.

He started running. The slap of his shoes on the treadmill beat a cautioning taunt in his head, *don't look, don't look.*

But he couldn't help himself. Shelley was flat out running at an incline. Her breasts bounced with each stride.

Her rich auburn hair had drifted from her pony tail to wisp around her face. A light sweat gleamed on her skin and her cheeks were already a little pink from the exertion.

But what drew him like a fucking moth to a porch light was her beaming smile. Her lips curved with happiness and her moss green eyes sparkled. Her joy at the simple fix nearly knocked him over.

"Oh my God." She huffed out her breath. "Thank you. I could totally bow down to you right now."

An image of her on her knees bowing for a completely different reason flashed in his brain. His cock reacted immediately to the carnal thought.

She must have realized how her words could be misconstrued because her face flushed bright red. "Um, you know, in thanks."

Ric snorted. He couldn't help it.

She wasn't trying to be suggestive.

"I'll just shut my mouth now," she said.

They ran in silence, the only sound in the heating room was the swish of the treadmill belts and the thud of their feet.

Shelley grabbed her water bottle and drank. Ric was mesmerized by the graceful arch of her neck. Now he was rhapsodizing over her neck. What the hell was wrong with him?

"This feels so good."

"You work out a lot?" he asked, thinking if he could get her talking he could ignore his body's reaction to watching her run.

"Most of my exercise comes from working on the farm. But I do try to get a run in a few times a week."

"Tell me more about the farm."

"I bought the land. I have several full time employees.

The rest are transient. But we grow the crops, harvest the produce, and then the crop yield goes to the food bank."

Ric watched as her face blossomed with animation. "Isn't that expensive?"

"It is but we've implemented a program where people adopt an acre. So they pay the operating costs."

"Smart."

"It's a fantastic program." She gestured with enthusiasm. "That's what the stupid article was supposed to be about."

"The article that prompted this whole thing?" Ric asked. "I thought it was a local piece."

"It was. Except it got picked up by a syndicated paper and things just sort of snowballed from there."

Kandi's companion had told the police that she'd seen the article about Shelley and gone completely wacko. She believed that she should have Shelley's money, Shelley's life.

"Although the original reporter," Shelley grimaced. "Skewed the article to be more about me and the Stone mansion, the farm and the program got some good publicity. Our donations are up."

Ric admired her dedication.

"So overall I'm happy." Shelley continued to run. "Really, I can't complain."

She took the extra attention on her personal life, and unexpected irritation of dealing with the stalkers, with grace. "Why aren't you more pissed?"

Shelley pressed the buttons to slow her pace. "My life is pretty damn amazing. I may have had some tough times but now I am grateful for every day and my healthy children and the ability to help other people."

Ric stopped his treadmill and hopped off. He grabbed one of the pristine white towels and rubbed down his face.

"You are extraordinary."

"How can I complain? I'm blessed," she said softly. Her eyes softened and her smile widened as her treadmill slowed to a halt. "But, thank you."

Yet whenever the subject came up she was more worried about her kids and their happiness.

Sweat gleamed over her skin.

"Trust me." Ric said, "Plenty of people complain." He tossed a clean towel to Shelley.

Shelley shrugged. "I feel sorry for people who don't ever find happiness."

After grabbing his weapon from the water cooler, he dropped onto a weight bench and straddled the black leather seat. "Do you ever think about your own happiness?"

"Not really." Shelley wiped the sweat from her face. "I just focus on other people. That brings me happiness."

Maybe that's why he had been discontent lately. She was making him think about things. Assess his life, assess his priorities.

He realized that being trapped in a hotel room with her had still been some of the best days of his life. In fact the last two days had been a revelation. He liked her. His restlessness in the hotel room had more to do with their incredible attraction than a desire to get away from her.

In fact, he didn't want to get away from her. He wanted to spend more time with her.

"I'd like to make you happy," Ric blurted out. Then felt incredibly stupid. She didn't need him to make her happy.

But he'd certainly like to try when this whole situation with Kandi was over.

Shelley's eyes widened in surprise and she stumbled as

she stepped off the treadmill. She appeared to gather her thoughts and then she visibly relaxed, smiled.

"I'd like that." The gleam in her eyes turned speculative. She gripped the ends of the towel in her fists as her gaze skimmed his body. He'd stripped off his t-shirt once he started really sweating leaving his chest bare.

"I can think of a way you could make me really happy." Shelley's smile was full of innuendo as she eye fucked him.

He laughed. "Shelley." His laugh broke when her gaze snagged on his steadily growing cock. Shit. No way to hide that while wearing his navy mesh basketball shorts.

Ric took a large gulp of water hoping to cool down his arousal, and his reaction to her blatant come on.

She was making him happy with just her words.

"I'd really like a happy ending." Shelley sauntered closer to where he sat.

Ric choked on the water and some trickled from his mouth and down his chin. She couldn't be saying what he thought she was…could she?

"That's really—"

"A great idea," she interrupted. "A fucking fantastic idea."

"What's gotten into you?" Ric raised his eyebrows totally trying to stall her, distract her, anything to keep his brain off what she wanted.

"Nothing today," she grumbled. "That's for damn sure."

Ric nearly choked again. He'd unleashed a monster. A sexed up, horny monster apparently.

She stalked closer. "How about a skinny dip?"

"I'm sure they frown on—"

"The only reason we had our suits on yesterday was because you were in the Aquavant room with us."

Ric swallowed again.

"So you want to…."

"Have sex in the hydro-spa pool."

Ric coughed again at her blunt, uncompromising words. "Pretty sure their patrons don't usually have sex in the pool." She stood in front of him now. Her legs straddled the weight bench and her hard nipples were level with his gaze. Her entire body radiated heat and arousal.

Slowly, so slowly, he had plenty of time to back away, or to push her away, Shelley lowered her body until she sat on his thighs. "Okay. You win."

Thank Christ.

"No sex in the pool."

His erection was harder than the barbell bar and about to burst from the elastic waist of his shorts.

"We'll just have sex right here," she whispered.

"Um, Shel."

Damn, but her sweet, toned ass sliding along his thighs was a special kind of torture. Before he could say another word, she pressed her palms to his cheeks and her lips brushed ever so lightly against his mouth.

Her bold tongue licked at the entrance as she rocked her hot pussy against his erection.

Fuck it. They were alone in the fitness center. There were no cameras. No one could get in.

Ric groaned into her mouth and when her tongue touched his, his control broke. He palmed her ass and rocked her harder into his cock. The heat from her sex seared him.

She ran her hands over his shoulders and down his pectorals exploring his skin with firm strokes.

He scraped her top up her body, the blade of his palm slid along her breastbone until he curved his hand around one exquisitely formed breast. Ric broke away from her erotic kiss and bent his head to taste the aroused bud.

He rolled her hardened nipple on his tongue like a sweet berry and he sucked. Hard.

Shelley moaned, her head tilted back, and her fingers gripped his shoulders like she was clinging to the side of a mountain and about to fall.

He speared his other hand beneath her shorts and along the smooth skin of her ass until he stroked her sex. Damn, she was soaking wet.

How could he resist her?

Shelley sat on Ric's thighs, his legs tightened beneath her ass. She marveled at the sculpted muscles of his chest. A smattering of black hair dusted his pectorals and lead in a happy trail down to the waistband of his basketball shorts. The bulge beneath the mesh was large, thick, and growing every second.

Her head went light when she thought about all that power inside her.

His biceps bunched, his brawny strength held in check as he tweaked her nipple with his callused fingers.

His cock pushed the waistband of his shorts and the purple mushroom head wept with pre-come. Shelley licked her lips.

Ric's scent mingled with the musk of their arousal and wafted in the air like a super charged aphrodisiac. She scraped her fingernails lightly along his scalp, triumph rose as he groaned into her mouth.

The last few days trapped in the hotel room with him had stoked her libido. She'd gone from an asexual being to becoming nearly obsessed with sex. Or maybe it was him. Maybe he brought out all these new, forbidden sensations in her. As if he was high-powered fertilizer, her sexual desire had grown from tiny to mammoth with every moment in his presence.

It wasn't just that. When he'd said he wanted to make her happy something had snapped to attention inside her. She was used to looking out for herself, making her own happiness. And if someone else tried, there was usually an end benefit for them. But there hadn't been any calculation in his gaze. No judging the effect of his words. He'd seemed almost surprised when he'd blurted out the statement.

He ripped her top over her head, the spandex caught on her ponytail holder, and her hair came tumbling down. Ric pulled his mouth away from hers. She sat on his lap, her bare breasts exposed to his gaze.

They definitely weren't as perky as they had been twenty years ago and while her abs weren't as tight either she thought she looked pretty good. She fought the urge to defend her body.

"Damn. You're gorgeous." If the expression on his face was indicative, he wasn't complaining.

With his index finger, he traced the blue vein that ran from her neck down to her breast. That one single point of contact was like a lightning strike, electricity shimmered over her skin. Her nipples tightened into nearly painful peaks.

Ric sucked, using his tongue to press the bud hard to the roof of his mouth. Sensation shot straight to her pussy.

She ached.

She wasn't sure what had come over her.

Her forced seclusion had stripped her of her power, stripped of her choice, and trapped in the hotel room with a man who wouldn't touch her and who she wasn't supposed to touch. She had been aching and aroused and frustrated beyond belief and all those sensations tumbled into a major break in her control.

She was a grown ass woman, and she wanted Ric Santana. Bad.

She knew he wanted her too. The spectacular bulge in his shorts had been a dead giveaway that the man wanted to have sex as desperately as she did.

She sat on the boards of multiple philanthropies. She'd raised four children mostly on her own. She'd faced down haters, jealous wives and mistresses, judgmental men, the bastard of them all Jackson Stone Sr., and she'd triumphed.

Two nights ago, she'd decided to throw years of reticence out the window.

At the time, she'd thought it was just a reaction to being here for the wedding. But if she were honest, she now believed that she was only having these feelings because of this man. There was something about him. About him and her together that was magic.

"I need you."

"Far be it for me to disappoint a lady," his voice was husky with arousal.

"I don't want to be a lady right now." She was tired of being a lady. Tired of trying to be the perfect citizen, the perfectly benevolent patroness. She'd spent years being polite, demure, above reproach, never making waves, never rocking the boat. She'd been that woman since she'd gone to live in the Stone mansion years ago.

And where had that gotten her?

Forty-five years old and she'd only had a handful of sexual partners. Until two nights ago she had never had multiple orgasms in a night. She'd never been so lost in another person she'd give anything to stay lost forever. Suddenly that lack seemed like an incredible waste of her life.

"I want to do everything," she told him enthusiastically.

"Everything?" But he didn't seem stoked, he seemed bewildered.

"Yes." Shelley thought about all the naughty things she'd read about or heard about when women talked in hushed voices at the country club, sometimes the same women who judged her for going to live with Jackson when Jess had been a little girl.

Bitches.

A thousand different images, sexual positions, sensual possibilities bombarded her brain. As if they'd been locked away behind her prim façade and with one simple sentence he'd released the floodgates. He wanted to make her happy.

"I want to go down on you." That's what would make her happy. Or at least it was a start.

Ric laughed. "I'm certainly not going to argue with you, but I'm not sure what you're getting at here *cariña*."

"I have years of sexual repression to make up for," Shelley said defiantly.

"Okay." But his actions had changed from sexual to comforting.

Forty-five and still a damn good girl. "Maybe you don't understand, but when I got pregnant I'd barely had a single orgasm."

Ric choked on his water.

"And then I had a baby at eighteen. My mother kicked me out."

"*Christos.*"

"I'm not telling you this for your sympathy," she said crossly. "I was trying to survive, not club hopping. And since I moved in with Jackson twenty years ago, I've had three lovers. Three boring older lovers."

Ric swallowed. In sexual years she was just a baby. "For years I've been the Queen of Lonely Hearts."

He brushed a tendril of hair from her cheek almost tenderly.

"Stop that. I don't want tender." She wanted hot, raunchy, dirty, nasty sex. "The other night was the most sexually explosive encounter of my life. And I don't want it to be a one off."

"Me either," he replied huskily.

"Make me scream."

CHAPTER 14

"*F*ar be it for me to deny you…anything."

She hadn't moved. Was barely breathing. "You'll—"

"Do whatever it takes to make you happy."

She eyed him speculatively. "So if I said I wanted to go down on you right now…."

Ric rocked up into her. "I'd say, I'd prefer to be inside you but it's your choice."

Her breath caught.

"Okay, we'll do that later."

"So what do you want now?"

"You," she said breathlessly. "I want you."

She burrowed her hands beneath the waistband of his shorts, shoving the material below his balls, and trapping his thighs. But he forgot all about the awkward when she wrapped her fingers around his cock. Her grip was tight, firm, erotic as she pumped his erection. "Gonna have to let go for a minute, sweetheart."

Her gaze was fixed on his cock, the head peeking between the gap in her fist.

Shit, if she kept this up it was going to be over before it started. "Stand up," he commanded.

Ric made sure his weapon was within reach and he still had a view of the only entrance to the room.

Shelley complied but she made sure to drag her breasts along his chest as she stood slowly. "You are so beautiful." He traced kisses up her abdomen and along the underside of her breasts.

Shelley curled her arms around his shoulder while his mouth played with her nipples.

Ric shoved her shorts to her ankles, trailing his palms along the back of her legs and down her calves. She shivered and he couldn't fucking wait to be inside her.

"Shit. Condom." Ric mentally reined himself in.

"It's okay." She breathed in his ear.

"I won't put you at risk." No way would he be responsible for another unplanned pregnancy.

Shelley stepped out of her shorts, grabbed the bright material, and withdrew a single package from the pocket. She ripped it open with trembling fingers.

The leather bench seat was cool beneath his bare ass. But he was burning up. He rubbed his fingers along her dripping wet sex while she tentatively rolled the condom down his erection.

"Still pretty amazing," she whispered.

"Yes, you are." He paused. Absolutely amazing.

"I was talking about how that fits inside me."

Ric wanted to shout with laughter but the awe in her gaze humbled him.

"You can take it."

"Maybe."

"Let's watch."

They bent their heads. Ric had never seen a more

beautiful sight than his cock sliding into her sex. Slow. Even. Every inch inside her and he seemed to swell harder, until he was buried balls deep. Her slick channel throbbed around him snug and sweet. The buzz in his body built as they sat still, neither moving.

Then she moaned. The sound was soft, erotic. "That feels so good." She nuzzled the skin behind his ear.

He took in the moment. The soft dim lights of the gym. The weight of her on his thighs. The snug clench of her sex around his cock. Her breasts pillowed his chest and her face nuzzled his neck. Her warm breath in his ear. The little sounds of her pleasure as she waited for him to satisfy her.

He felt like a god.

She'd blown his fucking mind.

How was that possible? He'd been around the world. Survived several tours with the SEALS, including some nasty places. And none of that had prepared him for the sweet, bombshell that was Shelley Stone.

Ric began to move, pressing his feet to the floor he pushed up into her, then rocked back. The head of his cock rubbed her g-spot, pushing her higher.

He swelled almost painfully tight. Desire built in the base of his spine.

They crashed into each other, her body strung taut. "Let go," he demanded. She bounced on top of him reaching for her pleasure.

Rick tilted her head and stared fiercely into her aroused, haze green eyes. "Let go," he demanded again.

With a noisy cry, she began to convulse. Her gaze went unfocused, and her lids drooped as her orgasm flowed over her entire body.

That was all it took for Ric to let go. His fingers bit into her hips as he held her still. The buzz at the base of his spine exploded outward and he began to come in long punishing pulses. Her pussy squeezed his cock, and his brain simply shut down.

Shelley's chest heaved and her breath soughed over him. She was slumped over his shoulder, barely moving. Little aftershocks sizzled beneath his skin. His cock was still semi-hard inside her, as they reveled in the mind-altering orgasm.

"Fuck me," he finally breathed out.

"Been there. Done that." She lifted her head, her eyes bright and her smile radiant. "Ready for round two."

He groaned. "Not here." They were out of condoms. And he wanted hours in a bed, taking his time to give her all those experiences she hungered for.

Ric's semi-hard cock slipped from her body. "We can clean up down here first." One of the pool rooms had a misting shower. "Then head back to the room."

"Okay."

They grabbed their clothes. Ric held her hand gently in his left. In his right, he carried his weapon.

"You really think you need that?" she asked.

"I won't leave you unprotected." Didn't matter if he thought he needed it. He didn't think Kandi was bright enough to evade the police for long but she'd proven to be pretty resourceful up to this point.

"I'll be quick," she said and headed for the shower.

"Go ahead. I'll be right back." He needed to dispose of the condom. Fortunately there were private bathrooms connected to the pool room. He would only be gone for a second.

Shelley finished rinsing off. She thought about waiting for Ric and standing under the water with him. But now that he wasn't right with her, doubts and insecurities came rushing back in. No need to highlight her body.

Besides, she was hoping she could convince him that they'd be safe in their hotel room if he stopped this overprotective need to guard her every second.

The cops should pick up Kandi soon. Right?

She pulled her running gear back on, then turned as she heard the door open, ready to greet him with a wide smile. She was going to have fun convincing Ric to do that again.

"Well, isn't this special?"

Shelley's heart thudded in her throat.

Shit. Kandi stood in the doorway. The gun in her hand was huge. Kandi didn't look so good. Her hair was disheveled and her tight jeans looked like they could use a washing. She still had on the heavy makeup from last night including the false eyelashes but her mouth was bare of lipstick and her eyes were wild.

Shelley could only be thankful that Ric was in the bathroom. Her heart beat erratically. She knew she needed to keep Kandi distracted. She didn't want Kandi suspicious of the fact that Shelley was in the spa by herself. She knew if she stalled long enough that she and Ric could overpower Kandi. Ric wouldn't let her down.

"What are you doing here, Kandi?"

That was the million dollar question. What did Kandi want? Because no matter how Shelley sliced it, she couldn't figure it out. She didn't really believe that Kandi wanted a relationship with Connor. She definitely wanted Shelley gone. But why?

"I want what I deserve." Kandi spat, "I've spent the last twenty-seven years slaving away, working my ass off, while you reaped the benefits of the Stone life of luxury."

"By life of luxury, you mean, wading through vomit when all four kids had the stomach flu? By going to parent teacher conferences alone and trying to figure out how to help the kids with their homework, making lunches, refereeing arguments? By living through their first broken hearts? The first time they came home drunk? The endless nights of worry of through their deployments?"

"Whatever." Kandi waved her hand, blithely dismissing Shelley's years of parenting. "I don't care about all that stuff."

Shelley was channeling 'be alert' vibes hard, hoping that Ric figured out something bad was going on.

The door to the bathroom opened. The squeak was barely, noticeable but Ric stopped cold when he saw Kandi and her gun. Kandi had her back to the bathroom door so hopefully she hadn't noticed him.

Shelley relaxed. Ric was here. After years of taking care of herself, she knew Ric wouldn't let anything happen to her. Shelley's job now was to keep Kandi distracted.

"I have a question. Why didn't you get an abortion?" She really wanted to know. "Don't get me wrong, Connor is a wonderful man and I'm really proud of him and I'm thrilled you didn't make that choice. But I'm guessing Jackson Sr. gave you money just like he did me."

"It's a sin." For an infinitesimal moment, Kandi looked lost. "I couldn't do that."

Huh, hadn't seen that one coming.

"But I couldn't raise a baby." Kandi stomped her foot. "Don't you see?"

"I see a selfish woman, who never thought beyond her own needs," Shelley sneered. Ric was almost at Kandi's back.

"Fuck you! You stole my life!" Kandi shouted. "I should be living in that house. And flying around in that private jet."

Ric hadn't taken his gaze off Kandi as he carefully eased

closer. But he lifted his brow so Shelley answered, "It's not really mine. But yes, the family has a private jet."

She just needed to distract Kandi for another minute and Ric would be close enough to disarm her.

Shelley said fiercely, "I will do anything for my kids."

"Connor isn't yours, he's mine." Like a kid playing tug of war with a toy, Kandi seemed stuck on claiming Connor.

"So what is it that you want Kandi?" Shelley asked softly.

"All you had to do was leave," Kandi said. "Why wouldn't you just go? I could have taken your place and everything would be perfect."

The woman had clearly lost her freaking mind. "What's the plan now?"

"I have to kill you," Kandi replied calmly.

"That doesn't really work for me," Shelley said in her most haughty Queen of the Manor voice.

"Whatever."

Shelley let her gaze slip to Ric. That was a mistake. Kandi stepped back and whirled, weapon up and steady in her hands.

Shit. Ric was close enough that he could lunge and overpower this crazy woman, but based on the confidence with which she held the weapon, she'd be able to get several shots off. At this range the damage would be considerable.

Now he remembered what had been bothering him. It had been Kandi's voice outside the door yesterday at the spa. But when they'd reviewed the security tapes, she hadn't been in the lobby area. Which meant that she had access to another way in to the spa. Which meant she had a contact within the hotel. Dammit.

Missing that detail had lead right to this moment.

Wasn't this irony? He'd spent almost twenty-five years in

the Navy and never been shot. He'd gotten dinged up plenty of other ways. Knives, shrapnel, burns, but he'd never taken a bullet.

That's why he'd been nicknamed Bulletproof. Now, retired from active duty and in the private sector, he was going to get shot by a gun-toting, crazy ass exotic dancer with a grudge against the Queen of the Junior League.

He laughed. The Universe had a wicked sense of humor.

"I am not funny," Kandi screeched.

"No. But you're going to ruin my perfect record." As he stood there, the light shone down around him from above. In that moment, he realized that to protect Shelley he'd lay down his life. He didn't care if he got shot.

"I don't know what you're talking about," Kandi cried.

Ric held perfectly still, trying hard to project an air of calm. He didn't want to do anything to rattle her.

He was going to have to move soon but he wanted more information before he got shot. "How did you get in here?" Ric asked.

"There's an employee entrance. You just have to know the security code on the door." She laughed. "Easy, peasy. I used to date a security guard here."

"You're smarter than you look," he injected every bit of admiration he could manage into his voice.

"Believe it or not," Kandi said proudly. "Connor didn't just get his smarts from his father."

As long as she kept the weapon trained on him he'd keep her talking. But he saw the resolution in her gaze and knew their time was up.

"Which means, I've got to wrap this up." She straightened her shoulders and aimed the weapon.

Ric bunched his thighs and launched himself at her. The report of the weapon was deafening in the tiled room.

Shelley screamed as Ric slammed into Kandi. He shoved her arms above her head, and the gun went off again. The bullet ricocheted around the room as he took her down, slamming her body to the tile floor. Her head thunked hard and her body slumped.

Then the pain hit. Blood obscured his vision and painted everything red.

Fuck. That hurt. His last thought was he needed a new nickname.

CHAPTER 15

It was over.

Kandi was in custody.

Ric had a nice, bright white bandage on his scalp and a new scar. But Shelley was safe. Not a scratch on her.

His suite was bursting with food and people. Platters of cheese and crackers, veggies and dip, and bottles of wine and beer sat on the wet bar. Shelley, Jack, Bliss, Jessica, Colin, Connor, Ava, Shane Washington, and Keisha Johnson were all jammed inside his room. Riley and Di were on their way in from the airport.

Everyone had a beverage while they munched on the snacks.

After two days of being trapped in this room and wanting nothing but to get out, Ric wished everyone would leave so he could be alone.

The adrenaline let down was kicking his ass hard.

Especially because he didn't want to be alone. He wanted to be alone *with Shelley*.

But somehow he didn't think her family would be on board with that. She was across the room on the sofa. Ric was resting on the bed, propped against the pillows. The furthest distance away from her as possible and about a million people between them. It wasn't his doing, so he figured it must be hers.

Jack was jabbering away about charges and evidence but suddenly Ric could feel the weight of her stare. On him. He met her gaze, held the intense connection and let everything he was feeling show.

He wanted all these people gone. Now.

Shelley shot up from the sofa. "Okay, everyone. Time to let Ric rest. Clear out."

Relief pushed hard.

It took another half an hour before the room was empty. The guys squeezed his hand and offered, 'I owe you's. The girls gave him hugs and thanks.

"If you're up for it. I could use your help on that other project I have going on." Jack shot a furtive look at Bliss but she was busy hugging Shelley.

"Happy to help." It was clear Jack still hadn't talked to his bride-to-be. "Let me know what I can do."

"Later, NLBP."

NLBP?

"No Longer Bulletproof."

Ric smothered a laugh. Especially since Shelley was glaring at Jack. Jack gave Ric a chin lift then headed out the door.

Connor was last. "You ever need *anything*, you ask."

Ric nodded, then groaned. The bullet had seared across his scalp. He'd been damn lucky. Since he'd refused the pain pills, it still hurt like hell.

Jess said, "You coming mom?"

"I'm good." Shelley crossed her arms over her chest. She was back in the yoga pants and top.

"But where are you going to…." Jess trailed
off. "Ohhh."

"I'll see you later," Shelley said firmly.

Thank God. Ric hadn't been sure that she'd been
planning to stay. Finally they were the only two left in
the room.

"I thought they'd never leave." Although her words were
confident, Ric could see the nervousness beneath her
surface.

Shelley hesitated then crawled on the bed to settle next
to him.

Ric pulled her closer. With her breasts cushioned against
his chest, he burrowed his fingers through her hair and
cupped her head in his palm.

He kissed her. Poured every bit of love and longing and
want boiling inside him into the caress.

Shelley broke away gently. "What?"

Of course, she wouldn't settle for nonverbal
communication. Luckily, after a life in the Navy, he was used
to having to spell things out in triplicate. "I'm crazy
about you."

She blushed.

It wasn't just a little pink in her cheeks either. The heat
traveled over her torso, shot up her neck, and flooded her
cheeks. He'd surprised her. Again.

"I'm too old to fall into, and fall for, insta love." Shelley
tried to deny their attraction.

So she thought it was okay to ask for sex, but not to
demand love?

"No, you're old enough to know when you see
something you want. Make the decision and then go for it."
Ric countered. "You've seen enough shit in your life to
recognize the real thing."

"It's too fast."

"Bullshit." Ric was not going to let her get away. "It's not fast enough."

Dammit, his body had recognized hers when she was sitting on that barstool two nights ago.

"I don't need anyone," Shelley said. "I've been taking care of myself for a long time."

He couldn't help it. His heart simply fell. What had he thought he could offer her? Nothing. She already had more money than she knew what to do with. A rewarding career with the farm. Her family, her kids.

"I know." But inside, he knew he had what she needed. He just had to convince her.

"But just because I can take care of myself doesn't mean it wouldn't be nice to have someone else looking out for me," Shelley said softly. "I knew you'd rescue me."

That belief in him was just one of the many things he loved about her.

"I want to be the one who makes sure you get the peace you deserve. To look out for you because you're too busy looking out for everyone else. To make you happy. To love you."

Shit, he'd done it. He'd actually used the L word.

"I…would like that." She dropped her forehead to his shoulder. "What if we're wrong?"

"Then we'll work on it." Ric had never felt more committed in his life. "But we aren't wrong."

She threaded the fingers of her right hand through his.

He couldn't believe he was having this conversation. "I didn't come here looking for this."

She snorted. "Me either."

"I know you didn't. You never think of yourself first."

Ric rubbed his palm of his left hand along the furrow in her spine.

"Having *your* life flash before *my* eyes changed my perspective." Shelley shivered. She shifted so that she was sitting on his lap and wrapped her arms tightly around his shoulders. They were twined together, comfortable and erotic, as if they'd been in this position a million times.

"We fit," she said softly.

"Like we were made for each other." Ric smiled. "Take a gamble on me."

Shelley said softly, "Okay."

"I, uh, don't have a lot of experience with relationships."

"Me, either."

He wanted to give her romance. He wanted to give her passion. He wanted to give her all the silly, impractical loving gestures that she'd missed out on before. He wanted to do things he'd never even considered. He wanted to fulfill every single fantasy she had and ones she hadn't even thought of yet.

As she lay on top of him, thinking about those fantasies, his cock began to harden.

"Really?" She laughed.

"What can I say? I told you I'm crazy about you."

Shelley's heart filled with joy. He was crazy about her. It was there in every look, in every gesture. His erection nudged at her butt. No way. She couldn't believe he was getting turned on now. "You have a concussion. The doctor said no physical exertion."

"I look at obstacles as opportunities."

"While I applaud your creative thinking and optimism, I'm not going to put you in any more danger today." She pressed a soft kiss to his lips, and savored the sweet, tender, loving embrace.

"There's always tomorrow."

"And the day after that." She rested her head on his chest and listened to his steady heartbeat. Contentment settled over her. She said firmly, "Tonight we'll use the opportunity to talk."

She bussed his forehead with a kiss and gave thanks that his reaction time was faster than Kandi's trigger finger. The Universe wouldn't have been so cruel as to give her Ric and then take him away. She needed to grab hold of every moment. No regrets. She might not be quite ready to use the word love but he should know how she felt. She inhaled, counted her blessings and made a life-changing admission. "I'm crazy about you too."

Ric's smile took her breath away. He squeezed her against his chest, his embrace sexy and comforting at the same time.

"Since I can't rock your world with mind-blowing sex," he paused.

Shelley waited, wondering what he'd say next. Anticipation shimmered in the air.

"I need a new nickname."

Shelley sat straight up and stared at him. *That's* what he wanted to talk about? He'd lost his mind. "You want to figure it out *now*?"

"Got to get it nailed down before NLBP sticks."

Shelley shuddered at the fact that he was no longer Bulletproof.

"I was thinking…K.O.S.H."

Ric's steady, calm heartbeat was suddenly super-charged and going a million beats a second. "KOSH?"

"King of Shelley's Heart." He carefully placed her palm over his thundering heart. "After all, you're the Queen of *my* Heart."

With that declaration, he managed to rock her world anyway.

CLICK here for the stunning conclusion to the Family Stone saga. Get ready for Jack and Bliss's wedding and John's story in Cold as Stone (John, Family Stone #7).

Thank you so much for reading Shelley and Ric's story! I hope you enjoyed reading Queen of Hearts as much as I loved writing this book. If you did enjoy this book, below are a few ways you can help a writer out!!

Good: Lend the book to a friend

Better: Recommend the book to your friends

Best: Leave a review at Amazon, BN, Goodreads, Google, Apple, Kobo…basically any place they sell eBooks. Every review helps my work get out to other readers and I cannot even express how much it means to me when you let people know you liked my work. Readers have so many choices nowadays and limited dollars to spend. It can be difficult to take a chance on a new author even if the premise sounds appealing. By reviewing books, you give other readers insight into the story world and help them make informed purchases.

Thank you, thank you, thank you for your support!!

p.s. Would you like to know when my next book is available? You can sign up for my new release email list/newsletter at Lisa's Confidants

DEDICATION

I loved writing Shelley's book. From the moment she
appeared on the page in Jess's book, I started thinking about
her. About all her sacrifices and the things she endured to
make sure her kids were launched into the world
successfully.

The traditional romance usually features characters in
their mid to late twenties, sometimes early thirties. The
construct behind that makes sense. It's a time when men and
women are ready to settle down and potentially have
children. It's logical. But what about all those women out
there who didn't get their happily ever after when they were
younger? Women and men don't shrivel up and die after age
thirty-five so why should romance characters? I loved that
both Shelley and Ric had some mileage on them but were
still open to the possibility of love. I hope you did too.

FAMILY STONE ROMANTIC SUSPENSE
SERIES

Stone Cold Heart:

Jess Stone, former FBI sniper, always felt like the kid who looked in the candy store window but could never afford to go in. But on a humanitarian mission to aid an earthquake ravaged country, finally she finds a place where she fits, in Colin Davies' arms, and working for Global Humanitarian Relief, her big brother's company. But can the former SAS thaw Jess's stone cold heart?

Carved in Stone:

Connor Stone has always been odd man out in his family. Not the oldest, not the most charming, he'd had a lock on the youngest until another half-sibling came to live with them, so he raised hell in his youth. Con knows now the only way to redeem himself is with deeds, not words and sets out to prove once and for all he is worthy of the Stone family. When his older brother asks him to take care of business, Con finally will have redemption he craves. Except when Ava Sanchez, his brother's assistant, is threatened, he must choose between saving the girl or protecting his family. Will his choice bring him love or break his heart?

Heart of Stone:

Riley Stone is the handsome brother, the charming one. Everyone who meets him compares him to his father, which in his mind is not a compliment. But he's never met a woman he couldn't charm, until he meets Di, an acerbic, smart-mouthed, passionate activist who has no time for him or his charm. On the run, in the midst of danger, the blistering passion they share explodes. Can these two opposites find common ground, or will Di smash Riley's stone heart?

Still the One:

Jack Stone, former Navy SEAL, and oldest Stone sibling is determined to keep his family strong. Family is everything. So he starts Global Humanitarian Relief and Stone Consulting to do some good and keep his family together. But when he has to team up with his old flame, Bliss, on a missing persons case, an evil threatens him, his family and the one woman he could never forget and doesn't want to let go. Can these two former lovers put aside past hurts and heal their hearts?

Jar of Hearts:

Prickly Keisha Johnson has the hots for Shane Washington. But she's not about to reveal her inner soft heart to the player pilot and open herself up to hurt, until a favor to their boss sends them undercover and under the covers. Can she trust his sensual attention or will he shatter her fragile heart?

Family Stone #1 Jess

In the early evening dusk, Jess Stone lay on her stomach in the twenty foot high rubble of a demolished church, underneath a black and gray city-scape tarp intended to camouflage her position. A sharp-edged chunk of debris dug into her lower rib cage, the scope of the Remington M24 cool and familiar against her face.

Her standard uniform of jeans, running shoes, and plain black t-shirt rendered her just another anonymous and transient relief worker...which she was actually. A black baseball cap hid her distinctive multi-hued blonde hair. The paper mask kept out the contaminated dust from the destroyed buildings but did little to stem the overwhelming stench of decaying bodies.

Tanks rumbled through the destroyed coastal town, their public address system blasting warnings for citizens to stay in their homes, curfew was in effect. The threat was a joke. Ninety percent of the people in the town didn't have homes left. Those who did were terrified to go back inside. In the fetid, humidity choked air, the tent cities erected in the parks and on the beach were seething masses of the injured and shock struck.

The substandard construction in the small country had never been enough to withstand the angry might of Mother Nature. Buildings had toppled like a stack of Tinkertoys, and left crumbling cement walls with twisted rebar poking out of the jagged ruins like a skeletal hand.

Trapped in the concrete pieces that littered the ground, the heat from the tropical day seared through her thin sturdy clothing. The stank of the raw sewage that ran in rivulets through the streets overpowered the salt-laden breeze off the ocean. People, covered with the grit of pulverized buildings and humans, shuffled along with blank vacant stares. Two weeks after the quake, still in shock, their lives decimated first by nature and then kicked and beaten by the ineffectiveness of a flawed relief system. Hundreds of humanitarian agencies had descended on the population duplicating efforts and yet completely missing the need in other areas. The government was ostensibly trying to coordinate the effort, however the mass chaos was undeniable.

Through the Leupold Ultra M3 fixed power sight, she tracked the movements of Henri LeRoy, leader of this tiny island nation, violator of human rights and dignity, and all around poor excuse for a human being.

Sickness roiled in her stomach. The power bar she'd eaten for breakfast threatened to add to the rubble pile as she tried to figure out how in the hell she'd ended up here. Back behind a sniper rifle with the power over life and death trembling in the muscles of her right trigger finger.

Dammit. When she'd decided to take control of her life and quit the FBI, she hadn't wanted to do this anymore.

She'd wanted to be a simple relief worker. She'd wanted to connect with her family, brothers and mother.

But that bitch, fate, had slapped her upside the head and now here she was, where she'd sworn she never wanted to be again. Looking through the scope of a high-powered rifle, with a crystal clear head shot and a murky sense of right and wrong.

With little fanfare, she could blast LeRoy's brain matter all over the silk-covered walls and the antique Louis the XIV scrolled chairs in the receiving room of his ridiculously elegant weekend mansion which, since built properly, had sustained minimal damage. Her muscles twitched with the knowledge and acceptance that with one slow slide of her finger, the despotic, amoral leader would be history.

Jess didn't want to kill him, didn't want to be directly responsible for another death. She didn't want this choice. She'd given up this kind of life. She'd left the FBI after a series of high stress cases to get away from the doubt and guilt that had crippled her. To make her own decisions about right and wrong rather than carry out the commands of her bosses.

But if Henri LeRoy lived, chances were astronomical that many other citizens would die.

And yeah, she'd probably been manipulated into this. Actually no probably about it. Assassination had not been listed as one of her duties when she'd joined Global Humanitarian Relief. Damn her brother anyway.

But now all she could do was lay here in the desecrated remains of the former church and hope that her special skill set wouldn't be needed.

Fortunately, she was secondary backup.

And unless several things went horribly wrong, she would break down her weapon, get back to the relief aid encampment, back to actually helping people, and be out of here without ever firing her rifle.

Then she could hand out seed packets to her heart's content and figure out what she was going to do next. If she'd stay with GHR and her brothers, or go. First, she had to get through the next two hours.

But if something did go wrong...she prayed that if she was called upon, she could make the right decision. Make the shot. Cold zero.

ALSO BY LISA HUGHEY

Black Cipher Files Romantic Suspense

The Encounter, A Prequel to Blowback

Blowback

Betrayals

Burned

Dangerous Game

**These books are also available in paperback

Black Cipher Files Box Set (includes Blowback, Betrayals, and Burned)

Snow Creek Christmas

Love on Main Street: A Snow Creek Christmas – 7 Author anthology

One Silent Night (from Love on Main Street)

Miracle on Main Street (standalone novella)

Family Stone Romantic Suspense

Stone Cold Heart, (Jess, Family Stone #1)

Carved in Stone (Connor, Family Stone #2)

Heart of Stone (Riley, Family Stone #3)

Still the One (Jack, Family Stone #4)

Jar of Hearts (Keisha & Shane, Family Stone #5)

Queen of Hearts (Shelley, Family Stone #6)

<u>Cold as Stone (John, Family Stone #7)</u>

<u>Family Stone Box Set (Stone Cold Heart, Carved in Stone, Heart of Stone, Still the One, & Jar of Hearts)</u>

<u>The Nostradamus Prophecies</u>

<u>View To A Kill #1</u>

<u>Never Say Never #2</u>

<u>ALIAS</u>

<u>Stalked (ALIAS #1)</u>

<u>Hunted (ALIAS #2)</u>

<u>Vanished (ALIAS #3)</u>

<u>Deceived (ALIAS #4)</u>

<u>Billionaire Breakfast Club</u>

His Semi-Charmed Life (Camp Firefly Falls #11 and Billionaire Breakfast Club #0)

Everything He Wants (Billionaire Breakfast Club #1 The Jock)

Queen of His Daydreams (Camp Firefly Falls #23 and Billionaire Breakfast Club #1.5)

Blowback (blo′ bak) *n.* A deadly, unintended consequence of a covert operation.

Eerie blue light penetrated my consciousness first. The regulated thump-thump of tires pounded in my head, echoing with fierce resonance.

Where the hell was I? Why did I feel like this? I kept my eyes closed, knowing pretense was paramount to my survival. Wherever I was, it wasn't normal.

Ha. My life would never be normal.

I tracked back to my last memory. I'd hooked up with a guy. Had relatively indiscriminate sex with him.

I inhaled shallowly, carefully, not wanting to give away anything. I still smelled like sex. Really great sex.

I wanted to smile but kept my expression lax.

I'd longed to stay in that bed. Sleep with him. Just sleep with the comforting warmth of another human being. The ache had been so intense that as soon as he dozed off--I left.

That was my last memory.

"You can stop pretending."

I continued to fake sleep. I didn't know that male voice.

It was bland, not angry, but with a slight smirk, as if he knew something I didn't.

"You should be awake by now. We calibrate our doses very carefully."

That statement raised so many questions, I decided to comply with his unspoken request and let my eyes drift open. I calculated we were moving at a speed of about thirty miles per hour. Suburban, blacked out windows, bulletproof glass. The blue light came from the interior dome in the big SUV.

"The light is to protect your eyes. The drug affects your pupil's ability to dilate and contract."

What drug? I kept silent.

"Not very curious, are you?"

My last conscious memory was from the motel off of 295 near Alexandria around nine in the evening. It was pitch dark out now, so I'd been out for a while.

Lucas. Could the guy have been a plant? Possible. Since he was my last clear memory, it made sense.

I sifted through the spaghetti of my brain. For the past two days, I'd been undercover, shadowing Staci Grant's life. Last night, I'd encountered Lucas Goodman, who'd been looking for Staci and thought he'd found her when he found me. The sexual heat between us had been instantaneous and mutual. A few sweaty hours later, I'd left, confident my movements as Staci had been tracked. My cover had been working.

They'd kidnapped Staci.

Excellent.

I was right where I needed to be.

Now I needed answers. My task was to discover why CIA, DIA, and NSA agents were being kidnapped, the method of interrogation, and who was doing the kidnapping. The answers would be coming. I just had to be ready.

I settled into the backseat of the car to wait, taking in details. Mistake number one. They hadn't taken my ring, so the satellite audio transmitter should work. I twisted the unusual ring with my thumb and pressed the citrine stone twice. I was now sending voice-activated recordings back to Carson.

Mistake number two. They'd cuffed my hands, in front, but left my legs unshackled.

They'd taken my government firearm but missed the knife in the sheath at my waist. Mistake number three. Always, always check everywhere for hidden weapons.

Although my mind was the most powerful weapon I had.

My watch was gone and my government-issue GPS with it. Slouching to the side, I got a better view of the dashboard panel. My kidnapper had conveniently supplied me with another GPS system, live and tracking.

Coordinates. Latitude–47. Longitude–122. I was in the Pacific Northwest. I looked out the misted window to see a reflection of the Space Needle and pinpointed my location as Seattle. I was a long way from Virginia.

I returned my gaze to the kidnapper. Subject was male, small head, blond hair gelled into little spikes, crescent-shaped birthmark below his right ear.

The car rolled to a stop. The rocking intensified my queasy stomach. I ignored it.

"We're here."

Here was a warehouse near the water. The guy wasn't rough but the sudden motion as he lugged me out of the SUV caused my stomach to roil.

I breathed in the cold, damp air through my nose, trying

to quell the nausea. As he led me toward a semi-truck trailer, I noted the parking lot was empty except for one other truck and a car, too far away and too dark to make out details. The warehouse, constructed with long cinder block walls interrupted by doors at twenty foot intervals, was to my left and behind me.

The trailer was modified from a regular shipping container, doors locked up tight in the back, with another entrance on the side. It looked as if the stairs were all one solid block which could fold up into the interior of the trailer.

The recessed entrance looked exactly like an old-fashioned front door complete with screen door. A porch light flicked on. The screen door wheezed open as a dark-haired woman in a white coat stepped out onto the platform.

The light behind her filled the doorway with shadows. I couldn't make out her features but I caught a furtive movement, the light illuminating her hand as she tucked a syringe into her pocket.

"Thank you. You can go now." She nodded regally to the man holding me. Her melodic voice held a hint of Asia, probably second-generation American.

He promptly let go of my arm and walked away. They must believe that the plastic restraint cuffs would be a big deterrent to resistance. The click of his heels echoed in the silence as she stared at me, her hands clasped tightly in front of her, so tightly her knuckles showed white.

There was something in her stance--tension, stress? I eased back a step.

"Welcome." She put a hand on the railing and took a step down. Then she hesitated and glanced back at the open doorway. "We won't hurt you."

I thought about the syringe in her pocket. *No thank you.*

I'd had drug resistance training but honestly I didn't want to put it to the test. At least, not yet. Although if that scenario became unavoidable and they pumped me full of drugs, the transmitter in my ring guaranteed I would get the information Carson and the NSA needed.

All of the kidnapped agents had an unidentified drug in their bloodstream and unknown consequences from those drugs. We had no idea what national secrets they'd given away or what kind of long-term effects were possible from the drug cocktail most likely in that syringe. My job was to get myself kidnapped, acquire the drugs, identify the perpetrators, and get out before they could accomplish their objective.

I wobbled as if unsteady on my feet and eased back two steps, assessing my position.

As the Suburban left, the beam from the head lamps shone on her. The shape of her face and the tilt of her eyes marked her as Chinese. Lines of strain curled around her mouth, the expression was supposed to be a smile but came off as more of a grimace. "Come with me."

I don't think so.

I'd expected the kidnapping, the intel suggested that Staci Grant would be next. I'd planned to resist at first. I didn't want to make it too easy for them to subdue me. Carson was supposed to have a team on standby waiting to capture the kidnappers after I completed my objectives. But since we hadn't planned for a cross country abduction— all of the other kidnappings had been local and accomplished within a matter of several hours—it would most likely take a little time before the extraction team got here.

If they got here.

I pivoted and ran for the warehouse door nearest me. Her footsteps rang on the metal steps as she followed.

"She's getting away." A man's shout, older, deeper, slightly frantic, registered as I reached the door. Two against one. More difficult, but not impossible. Woman, older man. Until I saw his physique, I couldn't judge who was more dangerous.

"I've got it," the woman replied and sprinted toward me.

I yanked on the handle, flung the door open, and slid inside. The heavy metal swung shut with an ominous clang.

Obviously, the drugs were making me melodramatic.

The warehouse was dimly lit. Industrial metal lights hung from the ceiling, their muted pink glow making the surroundings blurry. Metal shelving separated the concrete floor into long, wide aisles. Three tiers of jumbo shelves housed wooden pallets of goods. I stood at the end of one aisle.

I hustled over two aisles, pulling the knife from the sheath at my waist as I went. The restraint cuffs at my wrists took a few swipes before slicing clean through.

I grabbed some small ceramic rice bowls and shoved them into my jacket pockets. Mistake number four. They'd let me keep my jacket.

The door banged open.

"Don't let her escape." I could hear the man huffing, and a rhythmic thumping noise as they pursued.

"She won't escape," the woman replied grimly from somewhere behind me.

I stalked down the industrial cement aisle, my footsteps silent. Glancing around, I searched for another way out.

"Please don't try to escape, Agent Hunt." The man's plea had a desperate edge to it.

My legs faltered. I wanted to stop, stand rooted to the floor. Only training kept me moving.

He'd spoken my real name. My *real* name, not the cover I was using for this assignment. So who did they really want?

Me, Jamie Hunt, NSA agent? Or Staci Grant, CIA officer?

ACKNOWLEDGMENTS

No writer works in a vacuum. I am very fortunate to have a supportive group of writers and professionals behind me.

Huge thanks to Adrienne Bell, LGC Smith, and Cecilia Gray for pretty much everything and anything. A special shout out to Adrienne Bell for the ongoing word wars!! The Pens for being totally awesome-sauce, whether it be emergency pick-me-ups, or writing retreats at the haunted house, or impromptu sessions at Panera, or lunches at Buffalo Hot Wings.

To LJ at Mayhem Cover Creations. Thank you, thank you for the beautiful covers!

Thank you all. :)

ABOUT LISA

USA Today Bestselling Author Lisa Hughey started writing romance in the fourth grade. That particular story involved a prince and an engagement. Now, she writes about strong heroines who are perfectly capable of rescuing themselves and the heroes who love both their strength and their vulnerability. She pens romances of all types—suspense, paranormal, and contemporary—but at their heart, all her books celebrate the power of love.

She lives in Cape Ann Massachusetts with her fabulously supportive husband, two out of three awesome mostly-grown kids, and one somewhat grumpy cat.

Beach walks, hiking, and traveling are her favorite ways to pass the time when she isn't plotting new ways to get her characters to fall in love.

Lisa loves to hear from readers and has tons of places you can connect with her. It's a wonder she gets any writing done at all....

Sign Up for Lisa's Confidants
Visit Lisa on the Web

Follow Lisa's Boards on Pinterest
Follow Lisa on Instagram
Email Lisa
Be Lisa's Friend on Goodreads
Like Lisa on Facebook at Lisa Hughey: My Books

www.ingramcontent.com/pod-product-compliance
Lightning Source LLC
Chambersburg PA
CBHW050534190726
48284CB00003B/1061

9 781950 359004